Wrong Twin, Right Man

LAURIE CAMPBELL

SPECIAL EDITION

Published by Silhouette Books

America's Publisher of Contemporary Romance

Thanks to my gifted friends on the Desert Rose
brainstorming loop, who always come through
with new possibilities, and to Lori De Jong and
Mary Rahrig, who help me keep God in the picture.

 SILHOUETTE BOOKS

ISBN 0-373-24643-9

WRONG TWIN, RIGHT MAN

LAURIE CAMPBELL

spends her weekdays writing brochures, videos and commercial scripts for an advertising agency. At five o'clock she turns off her computer, waits thirty seconds, turns it on again and starts writing romance. Her other favorite activities include playing with her husband and son, teaching catechism class, counseling at a Phoenix mental health clinic and working with other writers. "People ask me how I find the time to do all that," Laurie says, "and I tell them it's easy. I never clean my house!" She rarely cleans her mailbox, either, which makes it a special treat to hear from readers on her Web site at www.bookLaurie.com.

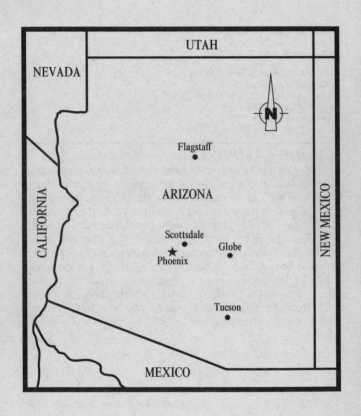

Chapter One

If only she could say he loved her, the toothpaste wouldn't matter.

Neither would the late hours. Neither would the baby—

No, the baby mattered.

"I want a baby," Beth told her sister. "It all comes back to that."

"Write it down," Anne ordered, turning over the dining-car flyer on their breakfast table and sliding the blank page across the white tablecloth. "If you want to straighten things out with Rafe, you need to know exactly what the problem is."

He doesn't love me!

But she couldn't bring herself to say that aloud.

"He doesn't want a baby," Beth said instead. Which amounted to the same thing. "I know we agreed to wait until the legal clinic was up and running, but that's taking a lot longer than I expected."

"Write it down," her twin repeated, handing over a pencil, and Beth dutifully jotted "doesn't want baby" on the paper. "When was the last time you talked about it?"

"Friday. The night before I left to meet you." The night before her and Anne's annual "Sisters' Vacation," she had accused her husband of caring more about Tucson's street kids than having kids of his own.

And he hadn't denied it.

"What happened?" Anne asked, and Beth gritted her teeth against the tip of the pencil.

"Nothing. I was kind of hoping he'd get mad, get upset, say I was wrong." If he had lost his temper, sworn at her in the same gutter-style Spanish he used with the former gangbangers who occasionally phoned the house, she could have taken comfort in knowing his emotions were fully engaged. "But he just said the clinic's not all the way there yet, and we have plenty of time."

"Twenty-six isn't exactly over the hill," her sister observed. "And Rafe's, what, twenty-eight? But okay, there's problem number one. What else?"

"Isn't that enough?" Beth protested, just as the waiter arrived with their breakfast order. She wished they could send him away, finish this conversation without the distraction of mushroom omelets and rye toast, but of course the fun of eating in a dining car was why they'd taken the train from Los Angeles back to Tucson.

Back to the husband who didn't want her.

Or at least not nearly as much as she wanted him.

"I still can't believe you decided to leave your wedding ring home," Anne told her, eyeing the *claddagh* ring she'd loaned Beth when she found her crying over the vacancy a few nights ago. "And didn't even mention it! Bethie, you need to talk about things more."

Maybe so, but she couldn't expect her sister to fix *her* problems. Taking care of people was Beth's strong point, while Anne took care of everything else.

Besides, she'd hoped that a week away from Rafe would settle the turmoil inside her.

"I just thought," she muttered, "I could try pretending we'd never gotten married, and see how it felt."

"But it feels sad, doesn't it?"

Which pretty well summed up her problem. Leaving the wedding ring in her jewelry box had been a foolish gesture, and the loan of her sister's ring hadn't made her finger feel any less forlorn.

"You have to talk things out," Anne continued. "Forget this new-look stuff, that's not what you need. Not that you don't look wonderful—"

"You're only saying that because I look like you."

Her sister grinned, acknowledging the point. With Beth's brand-new haircut, they looked more alike than they had in years. "Strawberry blondes are better with short curls, that's all there is to it. But anyway, talking to Rafe would be the fastest way to fix things. I mean, if you want to stay married."

"That's what's so embarrassing!" She still wanted him as her husband, and a whole week of vacation hadn't made any difference in that fierce, heartfelt yearning for Rafe Montoya. "What kind of woman wants a husband who doesn't *need* her?"

Anne hesitated, gazing at her coffee cup before meeting her gaze with an uncomfortable expression. "Bethie, I know you've got this thing about taking care of people, but being needed isn't the same thing as being loved."

Maybe such statements made sense for a career woman who didn't understand the essentials of love, but Anne was completely wrong. "That's what marriage is about!"

Her sister thought that over long enough for Beth to realize there was no comfortable solution to be found, then tapped the page on the table with her usual executive determination.

"You need a list of pros and cons," she announced. "Reasons to stay married, and reasons to get divorced. Come on, write it down."

"But…" What if the reasons for divorce outweighed the reasons for marriage? And how on earth had she and Anne traded roles so quickly, when normally she was the one taking care of her sister? "I don't want to give up on him yet."

"That goes in the pro column," Anne ordered, taking another sip of her coffee. "What else do you like about him?"

It wasn't a question of liking him, though. It was more a matter of loving him.

And suspecting he would never love her.

"Come on," her sister prompted. "Is he smart, handsome, rich, charming, good in bed—"

"Anne!" They were in the middle of a dining car,

with people all around them, and here she was asking about Rafe in bed?

''Good-looking, punctual, courteous, good athlete—''

''All of that,'' Beth interrupted hastily, trying to dismiss the memory of his athletic body pressed against hers. At least while making love to her, Rafe Montoya could be wonderfully free with his emotions. ''Well, except rich. He's still paying back his student loans, and the legal clinic won't ever make big money.''

''So that goes in the con column, along with waiting for a baby and leaving the lid off the toothpaste,'' Anne directed. ''Good thing he's punctual, though, if he's picking us up at the train station.''

They had arranged last week that Rafe would meet them at nine-thirty this morning, so he and Beth could show Anne their new house before taking her to the airport. And, knowing him, he had phoned the station at dawn to check on their arrival time.

Because while Rafe Montoya would never give his heart, neither would he give up a responsibility

''Probably coming right from work,'' Beth said, drawing a wavy line between the two columns on her page.

''He's at work this early?''

No hour was too early for a man whose workday could easily begin at three in the morning. Or last for seventy-two hours at a stretch...especially if a juvenile gang member needed someone to post bail, a ride home from the police station, or a temporary place to stay.

''He probably spent the night at Legalismo,'' she

explained. "I mean, with me on vacation, there's not much reason to come home."

But as soon as she heard the words "not much reason to come home," she wished she hadn't spoken. Because they sounded like a death knell for her marriage.

And she wasn't quite ready to accept that yet.

"Some people," Anne said dryly, "might think sleeping in a real bed was worth driving home for."

People who'd grown up sleeping in a real bed, yes.

"People like you and me," Beth agreed. "But you know how Rafe is."

Anne raised her eyebrows in agreement, as if confirming her initial opinion of Beth's husband. On the night of Beth and Rafe's engagement party, the first time she'd ever met him, she had drawn Beth aside and observed that the man was "incredibly gorgeous if you like that reformed-rogue, dark-and-dangerous look. But, Bethie, do you really want to spend the rest of your life with this Saint Rafael of the street kids?"

A question which had haunted her for the past six months.

"I know how Rafe is," Anne agreed, glancing at her wristwatch. "If you say he's gonna be on time, he's gonna be on time."

"You'll make your flight home just fine," Beth promised, noting with a touch of amusement that her sister was already slipping from vacation mode back into work mode.

Because she was still staring at her watch.

Or rather, at Beth's engraved confirmation gift, which Anne had borrowed on the first day of their trip. Leaving her own watch at home, Beth's twin had announced, was a stupid idea, and she was never listening to that stress-reduction tape again.

"Okay," Anne said now, looking up with an apologetic smile as if realizing how quickly she'd shifted gears. "So I'll be in Chicago by dark. But, listen, if you want time alone with Rafe, you don't have to give me the house tour yet. I can see it next time I come out."

"No, you have to see it! You'll love how I did the guest room like an office, and next time you visit it'll be like having your own desk right there."

Anne grinned at her. "Humor the workaholic, right? I did pretty good this week, though."

If you counted phoning the business manager twice a day as pretty good, then she had.

"You did," Beth agreed. "And we even found time for shopping." Her sister had insisted on new clothes to complement Beth's midvacation makeover at San Diego's trendiest salon, which had left them looking more like twins than they'd looked since seventh grade.

"Wasn't that fun? The waiter just now, I could tell, was dying to ask."

Anne always enjoyed fielding questions about what it was like to have an identical twin, and Beth had always been glad to let her sister do the talking. "You can tell him when he comes back with the coffee," she offered, returning her gaze to the list of pros and cons. "I wish we had another few days of vacation."

Sometimes a sympathetic look spoke more loudly than words, and Beth felt a flicker of dismay as she caught Anne's expression. Her sister evidently suspected that a few extra days of vacation wouldn't make any difference to the Montoyas' marriage, but she was too tactful for such an observation.

"Listen," Anne offered instead, "you know you can always come visit me. Actually, it'd be wonderful to have you looking out for things."

"What, at the office?" That wasn't Beth's domain, even though they shared ownership and responsibility for their nonprofit company. "I wouldn't know where to start."

"But you could learn. I mean, if you decide you want a change in your life."

Regardless of what happened with Rafe, though, she couldn't imagine trading roles with her five-minutes-older sister. Anne was born to run a Dolls-Like-Me business that had blossomed ever since she took it over, while Beth was happy to work at home, designing look-alike dolls for Down syndrome children.

"Not that big a change," she said. "But thanks, anyway."

"All right, then, think about your list. You've only got three hours to finish it."

Three hours to decide whether she wanted her marriage to last? "I can't decide anything that fast," Beth protested.

"You're not making any decisions yet," Anne explained, lifting her coffee cup and nodding at the waiter. "You're just listing the pros and cons."

"All right," she conceded, and as soon as the waiter returned for the kind of conversation that men everywhere seemed to enjoy with her sister, Beth set to work on her list.

There wasn't nearly enough space on the page,

though, to describe what had happened over the past two years. Ever since she'd turned over the management of her home-based business to Anne, who'd returned from Harvard with an MBA, Beth had been ready to start a family ahead of schedule.

And Rafe wasn't.

Not last year.

Not six months ago.

Not now.

No, all his passion was reserved for the legal clinic. All his fierce energy, all his intensity, all his time was devoted to helping kids escape the kind of life he'd survived with his crusading spirit aglow. The knight-in-shining-armor spirit which had captivated her the first time they'd met.

Back before she realized that it was far easier to *love* a knight in shining armor than to live with one.

"Tell you what," Anne said, jolting Beth out of her reverie as the waiter departed. "You look like you need a break. Let's go check out the observation car."

They hadn't toured the train last night, settling into their bunk-bedded sleeper compartment as soon as they'd pulled out of Los Angeles, but a view from the upper level would be a nice change of pace.

"Okay," Beth agreed, and folded her list in half. She stuffed it into the side pocket of her suitcase as they passed the luggage area, hoping that'd help her forget the entire problem.

At least for the last few hours of the trip.

After all, the whole point of a "Sisters' Vacation" was to enjoy spending time with her sister.

"Where shall we go next year?" she asked as they settled down in the observation car's last pair of upholstered seats, with a floor-to-ceiling view of the wide open desert. "It's your turn to pick."

"New York," Anne said immediately. "You've never been, and you're way overdue. Besides, if I'm still in touch with Marc, he'll get us tickets to any Broadway show we want."

Marc was the Italian architect her sister had met a few months ago, the latest in a string of eligible men whom Anne attracted and discarded with astonishing ease. But the idea of him being around next year implied more than the usual duration.

"You think he might be..." Beth hesitated, searching for the right word. "Is he special?"

"Not for a lifetime or anything," Anne said, handing the newspaper on the table between them to a passenger who had evidently been hoping for a seat. "But for a few months, I think he's a lot of fun."

If only she could borrow her sister's confidence as easily as she'd borrowed her *claddagh* ring. If only she could view the man in her life as "fun" and nothing more....

But that was no way to start a family!

And without a family, she might as well give up on mattering to anyone.

"You know what we need?" Anne asked, evidently noticing the distress on her face. "Coffee with brandy in it. Make the last part of the trip a little more bearable, what do you say?"

Coffee with brandy wouldn't make her homecoming any easier, Beth suspected, but if Anne was dreading the end of the trip, as well, it would be no problem to run down to the bar car.

"I'll get it," she offered, scanning the aisle and

realizing there were already passengers waiting for someone to leave. "If you want to save our seats, I'll be right back."

"Well, at least let me pay for it," Anne said, handing over her wallet-size purse and moving Beth's handbag into the empty chair beside her as a placeholder. "I'll be right here unless some better seats open up."

Such confidence was typical of her sister, Beth decided as she made her way down the narrow staircase with Anne's flame-red purse in hand. Some people were born with the kind of certainty it took to make things go exactly the way they wanted…which made them even more attractive to everyone they met.

And that observation was confirmed as soon as she reached the bar car, where a man with a briefcase looked up from one of the tables and greeted her with an exuberant smile.

"Anne Farrell! Jake Roth, from Boston. How've you been?"

She hadn't been mistaken for her sister since high school, and it was as disconcerting as ever. Flattering, yes, but also embarrassing when someone refused to believe they'd gotten the wrong twin.

Jake Roth was already standing up to shake hands, looking so pleased that she hated to disappoint him. "Actually," Beth began, "Anne is my—"

"Great to see you!" he interrupted, offering a hearty handshake before she could continue her explanation. "Mindy still asks about you, I've gotta tell her we were on the same train. Where you heading?"

"Uh, Tucson." It was hard to keep her balance, for

some reason, the train felt shakier than usual. "But, Mr. Roth—"

"Jake," he protested, when suddenly the floor jerked underfoot and Beth felt herself lurching sideways. He caught her, then stumbled himself, and the floor seemed to sway in the other direction.

She grabbed the table, which felt solid for a fleeting moment, until something slammed into the man beside her and sent them both staggering back. Then, as another passenger cried out in alarm, she heard a harsh, grinding shriek of metal and his warning shout, "Anne, hold on, we're gonna crash!"

No, surely they'd just hit a rock or something—but even as she fought for such reassurance there came a heart-wrenching scream. Beth froze in panic, felt the floor give way beneath her, and looked up to see the wall of the train collapsing on top of Jake.

And herself.

Would Beth be smiling?

Maybe, Rafe decided as he unlocked the scarred wooden door with its Legalismo sign, he should hold the flowers in plain sight when she got off the train. He'd stopped on his way to work for the kind of bouquet people gave visiting celebrities, a comparison she'd probably blush at...but he needed to show her how much she mattered.

After their grim parting last week, without even a phone call since her plane landed in California, he needed to prove to Beth she was still the most important person in his life.

So he'd made reservations for a homecoming dinner tonight, and—

"Hey."

The kid's voice was elaborately casual, but he recognized the desperation that would lead someone to camp outside a law office at this hour of the morning. And he'd be glad at any hour to talk with Oscar Ortiz, who reminded him so acutely of himself at fifteen.

"*Bueno,*" Rafe greeted him, then saw the gun in his waistband. Rather than risk losing the kid again, he made a show of fighting a yawn. "I was just thinking about getting some coffee. Walk with me?"

He wouldn't mind a cup of coffee in spite of the August heat, because as long as they stayed on the street he could avoid enforcing the No Drugs/No Weapons policy that ruled the clinic. So when Oscar shrugged, he locked the door and started down the cracked sidewalk toward the nearest bodega.

If he could ease Oscar out of Los Lobos the same way he'd gotten himself out of the Bloods...

"You still lookin' to meet Cholo?" the boy asked, and Rafe shot a quick glance at his watch. This could be tight, because he had to leave for the train station in plenty of time to meet Beth. Yet he couldn't ignore the chance to strengthen a potential bond with the leader of the second biggest gang in the area.

Oscar evidently saw the glance, though, because he immediately withdrew the offer. "Lawyer's got places to be."

"Yeah," Rafe said. No sense trying to save the conversation now, and as long as he kept things straightforward there might be another chance later. "I'm picking up my wife. She's taking the train in from L.A."

The kid gave him a suspicious glance, even as he

swiped his hand across a bench with a rival gang's chalk-marked emblem. "That's not the one that crashed, is it?"

A train crash? No, he would've heard.

"It was on the radio," Oscar reported, evidently seeing his disbelief. "Some big wreck out in the desert."

No. Not Beth's train. There had to be, what, half a dozen trains between here and Los Angeles? More than that. There had to be.

But even so, he felt a cramp of fear in his chest before reminding himself that Beth was surely fine, that he wasn't losing anyone he loved.

Not again.

Never again.

"She can't be on that train," Rafe told Oscar, who shrugged and looked past him toward the police car at the corner. "Not Beth." Not his wife. "She's fine."

The kid shrugged again, as if unwilling to comment, and Rafe felt his body tightening with the same reflex he used to feel before an attack.

"It's a mistake, that's all," he said. The radio probably reported things wrong all the time, and some station must've been trying to stir up excitement by announcing a train wreck that had never taken place. "I just need to straighten it out." A simple phone call would do the trick, and for the first time he found himself wishing he'd given in to Beth's request that he carry a phone for those nights he worked late.

"The radio—" Oscar began, and Rafe cut him off.

"I've gotta find out what happened." There, a pay phone across the street. No one there, either, which—

if the phone still worked—would save him the two minutes it'd take to run back to the office. He sprinted for the phone and felt a surge of relief at the sound of a dial tone, then fumbled in his pocket for change.

Beth was fine.

He just had to—

Damn! Two nickels and a couple of bills, which meant he'd have to hit the bodega for change and then—

"Here." Oscar dropped a handful of coins on the ledge beside him, then sauntered away as Rafe fumbled with the quarters. Where to call, somebody, who, the train station? Right, they would know, and from memory he dialed the number he'd called at dawn to confirm the nine-thirty arrival from Los Angeles.

Somebody *had* to know, he told himself as he listened to the phone ring. Somebody there would tell him everything was fine, that Beth was fine—she had to be fine, he wasn't losing her. She had to be safe.

"The nine-thirty from Los Angeles," Rafe barked at the clerk who answered the phone. "My wife is on there, and—"

"Sir," came the reply, "there's been a…a delay…and we'll have all the information here. If you'll please come—"

"No, I just need to know, is she all right?"

A hesitation.

"Sir, please come to the station and—"

He slammed down the phone. This wasn't working, but everything would be fine. *Beth* would be fine. Okay, maybe they were having some problems, but he could fix that. Get everything straightened out, make her understand they still had plenty of time for a baby. He could fix anything, he just needed to find out what was—who could—

Morton, he remembered. The cop who'd helped him, under the radar, a few months ago when those kids needed a word.

Morton could find out. Except, damn it, he'd left the number back at the office.

Rafe took off running, fueled by the same panic that had once filled his nights as a matter of routine, back when you never knew who was coming after you. Nobody after him now, the streets were almost empty—although that didn't necessarily mean anything—but all he had to do was reach the clinic, fumble with the door key, shaking, damn it! and there was nobody waiting for him, good, because he couldn't protect anyone else right now, not until he found Beth.

There, the phone. Morton's number, direct line, if the cop would just pick *up,* okay, no time for conversation, just identify himself and ask—

"Can you find out about a train wreck?"

"What, the derailment?" The cop's voice was more curious than bewildered, which meant Oscar's radio report might've been accurate after all. But that still didn't mean there was anything wrong. Beth was fine.

"The one from Los Angeles," Rafe said over a short, tight breath. "My wife's on there."

"Oh, man." Morton sounded alarmed, but that was probably just the phone connection. Because everything was fine. "Hold on, let me see what—hold on."

Beth was fine, he repeated to himself as he gripped

the phone with a fist too numb to release, and paced the six-foot gap between his desk and the door.

Beth was safe.

She was on her way home right now.

Right. Right, although people didn't always come home—look at Mom, look at Carlos, look at Nita and Gramp and Rose—but this wasn't the same thing. It wasn't like he depended on Beth.

Never had, never would.

So she had to be fine. It was just taking Morton a while to confirm that, but any minute he'd be back on the line with word that Beth's train delay was nothing, a minor glitch…. And there he was now.

"Rafe?" The cop sounded uneasy, and he felt himself bracing for a blow before he could remember that everything was fine. "Look, I'm sorry to have to tell you this, but—" Then Morton broke off. "Wait a minute, was your wife traveling with—"

"Her sister, yeah," he managed to answer. Maybe there was a mix-up, maybe something had happened to her sister. Which would be hard on Beth, yeah, but as long as she was still alive— "Anne. They're twins."

"Ah, hell," the cop muttered. There was a pause, during which Rafe scrambled for any prayer he could think of, any hope, any magic, and came up completely blank. "The sister's being transported to emergency right now. But Beth…I'm sorry. She didn't make it."

No.

No, he repeated as he slowly replaced the phone in its cradle. That wasn't possible.

It couldn't happen.

It happens all the time.

No.

Not this time.

"She didn't make it."

Not Beth.

Not again.

But already he recognized the feeling—that same heaviness, that same hot pressure of tears—

No.

No tears. He had to move, Rafe knew, he had to move someplace, do something—

Not cry.

No. No point. He stumbled into the lobby, where if anyone was waiting he could find something to do, something besides crying, because he wasn't crying, this was crazy, even with nobody here he still wasn't breaking down—

It hurts.

No, it couldn't. Beth couldn't be gone, because he still needed to fix things. After the way she'd left, thinking that delaying a baby meant he didn't love her, when he *did* love her—

But not enough.

Never enough.

Rafe felt a shudder rising in his chest and gulped it down, bracing his hands against the back of the cracked plastic sofa where clients waited for the lawyer on duty. He couldn't lock the door, not when someone might show up any minute, but he couldn't—

God, he couldn't do this.

He couldn't fix this.

He *had* to fix this! That was his job, fixing things,

and he couldn't stand here crying in the clinic lobby—

But the tears wouldn't stop. No matter how he clenched his muscles, how rigidly he held his breath, for some reason there was no swallowing the—

Not here!

Rafe fled to the bathroom and slammed the door lock home, already feeling the torrent of heat swelling into his eyes, his throat. God, he was practically choking, and suddenly he was sobbing, and somehow he couldn't seem to stop, couldn't keep from gasping out the desperate plea....

No. Not Beth.

Not this time.

Please!

There was no answer, which he already knew was the only possible response, but even so he begged with all his heart, with all his hope, knowing all the while that it wasn't enough. Crying wouldn't help, nothing helped, and he had to get himself together, get himself out of here, get back to the kind of strength he'd spent a lifetime building so this pain would never come back.

It was back now, though, worse than he remembered from the last time, although by now he knew how to fight it. Knew how to move, knew to flex his arms behind his back, to stop those bone-jarring gasps for breath and count five, ten, fifteen...

Seventy-five, eighty, eighty-five.

Two twenty, two twenty-five, two hundred thirty.

Counting as high as it took. That was the beginning, he knew, but real strength lay elsewhere. For real strength, he had to get out of here, he had to take care of someone. Anyone. Maybe some clients in the lobby, although he hadn't heard anyone come in—and when he finally managed to square his shoulders and resolutely opened the bathroom door, the clinic was empty.

Okay. He could still get through this.

He knew what to do.

If there was nobody here, he'd try somewhere else. He could do it, Rafe knew. He'd done this before. Just find someone to look out for, somebody hurting or scared or—

Hurting. Right.

Anne.

Emergency, the cop had said, and she'd have to be at the hospital by now. So...

Okay. He locked the clinic door for the second time that morning and started for the dirt lot behind the building. Just move, just go. Protecting someone was the key to staying strong, and Beth's sister was probably in bad shape right now.

So get going, Rafe ordered himself, stumbling blindly toward his car. Go, and you can get through this.

You can do this.

Go take care of Anne.

Chapter Two

"Anne? There's someone here to see you."

The soothing voice was familiar, although she couldn't quite say why. Maybe she'd heard it this morning, or during the night, or—

Wait, was it morning?

Well, there seemed to be light somewhere, yes. And the light seemed familiar, as well, which must mean she was at home in—

In—

In bed, right, but why didn't this feel like her bed? Her bed shouldn't hurt, yet this one felt strangely painful. Like she'd been sleeping wrong, with her arm twisted backward and something burning her side.

"Anne, would you like to visit with your brother-in-law today?"

The question sounded like it was meant for her, but

did that mean she was Anne? The name seemed familiar, somehow, even more than the cajoling voice and the light creeping into her eyes....

"He's been coming every day to see how you're doing, and he keeps saying you're not to worry about a thing—"

"Okay," she murmured. Or at least she meant to say that, but her voice didn't sound quite right. Still, it must have gotten through to the woman who was speaking, because she gave a delighted cry.

"You're awake! Let me run tell Dr. Sibley. Now, you don't have to see anyone until you're ready, but I know your brother-in-law would be thrilled if you're feeling up to it."

"Okay," she said again, and this time it sounded clearer—even though she still couldn't quite sit up. "What... Uh, what..." She couldn't quite think of what she wanted to ask, but something didn't feel right.

"You're in the hospital, sweetie. You've been here for eight days, and we were starting to get a little worried about you, but now you're going to be just fine."

The hospital? Had they taken her tonsils out? She remembered the hospital, with her sister in the next bed—oh, and they were laughing about something!—but that seemed like a long time ago. Eight days?

No, more than that.

"I'm going to send him in," the woman announced, helping her to a sitting position that somehow rattled a tube in her arm. "You take all the time you want to get comfortable, and he's certainly not going to expect any conversation, but if Dr. Sibley is on rounds you might as well have some company with you."

"Okay." She was getting pretty good at that one word, and it seemed to thrill the nurse—a nurse, right? Wearing a white uniform in a hospital, she had to be a nurse. And the way she backed out of the room, with a watchful eye all the way to the door, rang with the comfort of familiarity.

Even if everything else was mixed up right now, at least she could still recognize a nurse.

She didn't recognize the man who came in next, though. Not a doctor, because he wore what she thought of as "lawyer" clothes—a conservative white shirt and gray suit, but with his tie and shirt collar loosened.

And he also wore a look of intense relief.

"Anne," he greeted her, reaching for both her hands and giving them a surprisingly gentle squeeze. Maybe because of that metal thing bracing her arm, which she didn't remember from the tonsil hospital. "You're gonna be okay. Dr. Sibley said another few days here, maybe six weeks of physical therapy, and you'll be good as new."

He seemed so pleased about that, it must be good news. "Good," she managed to answer. But it didn't explain who this man was. "Um…are you the doctor?"

He reacted with a jolt of shock as he moved a plastic chair closer to her bedside, then she saw his startled expression replaced by something more careful. More calm.

"I'm Rafe Montoya," he said, and hesitated. As if

he was waiting for her to recognize the name. "Your sister's husband."

Her sister had a husband? She hadn't remembered *that* from the tonsil hospital, either, but if her sister was married they must have left childhood behind them a long time ago. "Where is she?"

Even though the man retained that same relaxed demeanor, she saw a flash of pain in his eyes before he sat down and met her gaze again. "She isn't here. You...you were pretty badly hurt."

"I thought so," she admitted, shifting away from whatever was pressing against her side. "I don't feel right."

He nodded, then reached across her to move something at the edge of her bed—which left her feeling a little more comfortable. "You and Beth," he said slowly, "were in a train wreck."

"Beth?" That name felt familiar, and from the way he spoke it, she could tell it belonged to someone he loved. "My sister?"

"Yeah. Anne, I'm sorry." The nurse had called her that, too, which meant she must be Anne. And the combination of those names seemed to resonate within her, as if Anne and Beth belonged together. "I didn't realize you— Everything's kind of a blank, huh?"

Pretty much, but she hated to see this man so worried. Especially when he had his wife to worry about...although Beth must be all right by now, because otherwise her husband wouldn't be here.

"No," she assured him, "I remember having our tonsils out." For some reason that memory was the clearest—maybe because this hospital smelled the same as that other one—but there were other images floating in her mind, as well. Playing with a dog, braiding each other's hair, cutting out snowflakes... "Only it was a long time ago."

"Yeah, I guess it was." He gazed at her for a moment, as if the sight of her face offered some curious mixture of nostalgia and regret, then gave her an apologetic smile. "Look, maybe you just need to concentrate on getting some rest. There's a lot of people praying for you."

"Really?" For some reason, she couldn't think of anyone who'd do that except her sister, who ought to be arriving any minute...because somehow she had the feeling there was no other family in her life. No parents, no grandparents, no one but her sister.

And this man. Rafe.

Her sister's husband.

"Yeah, well, Jake Roth—the guy who pulled you off the train?" Rafe seemed to think that phrase might trigger a memory, but again nothing came to mind. "He and his wife have been calling. And everybody in Chicago."

Chicago. That sounded vaguely familiar, and she had an impression of a city skyline. Maybe on a calendar, or a postcard. "Is that here?"

"No, right now you're in Tucson." He closed his eyes for a moment, then continued, "That's where Beth and I lived...uh, live." But the falter in his voice spoke more vividly than his show of calm, and she knew there was something terribly wrong. "You and Beth were on vacation, and—"

"Is she okay?"

He hesitated, and she felt a sinking sensation inside

her even before he met her gaze and said quietly, "Beth is...she's gone."

Gone? As in—

She must have flinched, made some kind of whimper, because he swiftly reached for her hands. "Anne, I'm sorry," he blurted, then continued in a rush as if the right words delivered quickly enough could somehow ease the shock. "Everybody said it must've happened really fast, before the fire. She never knew what hit her."

But that meant—

"Beth...my sister? She's dead?"

Still holding her hands, he nodded. Just once, without looking up.

"Oh, no." That couldn't be. "No, she's not." Only a moment ago they'd been playing in the tonsil hospital, arranging paper dolls on their beds, and— "Not my sister!"

But his expression didn't change, and she felt a new jolt of pain that eclipsed any other sensation. Her other self, her longest companion, the sister she'd shared her life with was gone?

No, she couldn't lose her sister.

"I can't—" she began, then stopped. Crying now would only make the pain worse, and she couldn't bear that right now. "Oh, Rafe..."

"I'm sorry," he repeated, with a crack in his voice, and suddenly she realized that he must be hurting as much as herself. This ache, this sharp and hollow desolation, wasn't solely her own...but how was anyone supposed to get through a loss like this?

She couldn't think about it, that's all. Surely the next time she woke up, her sister would be in the bed next to hers. All she had to do was sleep again, and everything would be fine.

Except somehow she knew it wouldn't be. Maybe just because of his anguished expression, but—

Oh, dear God. Not only had she lost her sister, but this man had lost his wife.

"Are you okay?" she blurted.

The question seemed to startle him, because he let go of her hands and sat up straighter in his chair.

"I've had a while to get used to it," he answered with such deliberate steadiness that she knew he *wasn't* okay, but that he wasn't about to say so. "Anyway, I know Beth would want me to make sure you're all right."

Which explained why he'd been coming every day for the past eight days. Beth must have wanted the certainty that her loved ones were taken care of.

"Anything you need," Rafe continued. "The insurance and everything, I took care of that already. But anything else...I want to help." And then, as if he knew at the same moment she did that nothing sounded better than sleep, he stood up and shoved his hands into his pockets. "I mean it, Anne. Whatever you need, I'm here for you."

He did mean it, she knew, even before he rested a gentle hand on her shoulder and turned to move his chair away. And she knew why it mattered to him... which meant she must be remembering the essence of her sister.

"Someone has to be there for the people she loved," Anne whispered. Because somehow she already knew that, even while Rafe was looking out for her, she needed to be there for *him*, as well. "That's how Beth would want it."

That's how Beth would want it.

The phrase stayed with him over the next few days, promising a faint hope of making amends to his wife. If he could just continue taking care of Anne until she was back on her feet, he could take comfort in knowing Beth's wish was coming true.

At least one wish.

"Feeling better?" he asked Anne each afternoon for the next week, and her responses grew gradually more coherent. To the point where he could finally tell her, "The nurse says you'll be ready to leave, day after tomorrow."

"I can't wait to get out of here," she said, shifting in bed with considerably more ease than she'd shown only a few days ago. "Back to…well, real life."

But she looked uncertain about the prospect, which he suspected meant there were still some gaps in her memory.

"Look, don't push yourself," Rafe warned. He'd already phoned Dolls-Like-Me to warn everyone that Anne needed time to recover, and had accepted their condolences with the careful guard he'd perfected over the past two weeks. "If it takes a while for you to remember things, the doctor said that's normal."

"I know, but I hate not knowing things! Yesterday someone named Marc sent this strange letter saying he wants to give his marriage another try. Except I can't believe I'd be dating a married man."

He had no idea who this woman might date, but she seemed so disturbed that he hurried to offer the first reassurance he could think of. "Maybe the guy didn't tell you he was married."

Anne contradicted him with a rueful smile. "Or maybe I'm a really bad judge of character."

No, that didn't fit with what he knew of her. "Beth always said," he offered over the knot that still rose in his throat whenever he spoke her name without preparing for it, "there was nobody in the world as smart as you."

Without warning, he saw her eyes fill with tears. But unlike himself, she seemed to take such weakness for granted.

"More than anything," Anne whispered, "I miss *her*. I don't remember what we used to talk about, or even her phone number, but I remember having the other half of me. I can't believe she's gone!"

Losing someone you'd known since before birth, he realized, must be even more traumatic than losing your memory. And while time supposedly made every loss better, you sure couldn't prove that by him.

But he was fine, Rafe reminded himself hastily.

He knew how to get through this.

"If only I'd stayed with her," she continued, twisting the edge of the hospital sheet between her fingers. "If we'd been together when the train crashed—"

"You're not blaming yourself, are you?" he interrupted. He'd done the same thing when Gramp died, and again when Carlos was shot, but she couldn't possibly be responsible for a train wreck. "It was an accident, Anne. One in a million."

"I just...I wish I'd done something different. I don't know what," she said, and her voice broke on the edge of a sob. ''But to let my sister die, and not me…that's not right. It's just not right!''

Her loss was even worse than his own, Rafe realized with a tug of compassion. Maybe he was hurting, but at least he knew how to take care of himself. ''I'm sorry,'' he said, leaning forward to take her hands in his. ''I'm really, really sorry.''

Her tears spilled over so easily that he found himself almost envying her—which was crazy, because this woman didn't have anything to fall back on. Nobody to protect. But after a few minutes, she straightened up and wiped her eyes, looking so much like Beth that he felt his heart twist all over again.

''I shouldn't keep—'' she began apologetically, then broke off. ''You're going through the same thing.''

Not exactly, because Anne had never failed the sister she loved. Never woken up reaching for Beth before remembering, once again, how cold and how distant their parting had been.

But there was no point getting into any of that, no point in encouraging her sympathy.

He didn't need it.

''Yeah,'' Rafe muttered, ''but at least *I* can remember where I live.''

She gave him a startled glance, and then the same wry smile he'd seen on Beth a thousand times—making his heart lurch for a moment before he realized that identical twins would naturally share similar expressions. Seeing Anne's smile, though, he was struck once again by the astonishing resemblance between the sisters, and for a wild instant he wondered whether there could have been some mistake.

But an old friend had identified Anne to the trauma team, and they'd reported finding Beth's watch and handbag with her body. Besides, this woman's hair was different and the ring she wore wasn't Beth's... which meant, Rafe knew, he was spinning impossible fantasies.

"I sort of remember where I live," Anne told him. "And I know, once I see it, everything will come back. I just need to get home, and the hospital social worker's coming to talk about that tomorrow."

But his phone calls to Chicago had revealed that Beth's original assessment of Anne was correct. As a woman completely dedicated to business, she'd never bothered with close friendships.

At least not with the kind of friends who would take her in while she completed six weeks of physical therapy. Everyone who'd inquired about her had sounded cordial yet harried, and not one had offered her a place to stay.

The way Beth would have, in an instant.

"Look," he said, "before you talk to the social worker, there's something I want to run by you. Because while you're doing your physical therapy, you'll need a place to stay."

"I have an apartment in Chicago," she told him, then gestured toward a small red purse on her bedside table. "I keep looking through my wallet for clues, and I live at—"

"Yeah, but you need a place where there's someone to look after you." Maybe not around the clock, but at least someone who could be on call throughout her recovery period. "I think you should stay in our guest room," he told her. "I can drive you wherever you need to be, or you can use Beth's car as soon as you're driving again. And anything you need help with, I'll be right there.''

She looked a little hesitant. "I…"

"Or if I'm working," Rafe continued hastily, "I'll have the phone with me." The phone Beth had urged him to use, and though he hadn't honored her request at the time he could damn sure make up for it now. "You can call anytime. Anytime. I mean it."

Anne regarded him with a sober gaze. "You've put a lot of thought into this," she observed.

Because it was his only way of making amends to Beth. The only possible way to keep himself strong. To protect someone who needed it—and she *did* need it.

"Well, it just makes sense," he said. "For the next six weeks, I think this would be the best thing for you."

"Maybe it'd bc the best thing for both of us," she said, which startled him. Anne didn't need to worry about what was best for him.

But as long as she was willing to let him take care of her, Rafe reminded himself, there was no point arguing about it. And already she was nodding in agreement.

"All right, then. Thanks," she murmured, and he felt a rush of relief shoot through his veins. "For the next six weeks, Rafe, I'll come stay with you."

Rafe was as thoughtful a host as anyone could possibly want, Anne decided after he'd left her alone to "settle in" to the guest room Beth had reportedly decorated with her in mind. The room wasn't quite as cozy or relaxing as she might have liked, but surely her sister had known her tastes.

Which meant, she realized while rearranging the bewildering jumble of faxes on the desk, this room was just one more example of how the accident had changed her character.

It was nothing to worry about, Dr. Sibley had assured her. People always changed after some kind of trauma, and the changes seldom lasted.

So this feeling of being slightly off balance, of not recognizing clients and names she had apparently known for years, was sure to disappear soon.

As if he'd sensed her disquiet, Rafe called from the hallway outside her door, "Anne, you all right? Can I get you anything?"

"I'm okay," she called back, then realized he must be deliberately keeping out of her room. "Come in...I was just looking at all these faxes."

He frowned when he saw her hunched over the desk, but refrained from comment. Instead he said, "I'm going to make some coffee, if you want any."

Coffee sounded surprisingly good, although she hated to have him waiting on her after he'd already disrupted his entire day to bring her home from the hospital, past the physical therapy clinic for a first meeting with Cindy, and finally here.

"I'll do it," Anne offered, and he stopped her with a quick gesture.

"You'll be on your own tomorrow morning, remember? Don't push it."

She had insisted that he maintain his usual schedule at the legal clinic, even though it meant taking a cab to her therapy session, and Rafe had reluctantly agreed to keep his early-morning appointment with a pregnant teenager. This man *lived* for the street kids he served, Anne suspected, and her rueful awareness of such devotion meant that Beth must have complained about it.

As a third party, though, she couldn't help admiring his heartfelt dedication to the job.

After all, from the tone of the messages on her desk, she apparently shared it herself. Which made it all the more disturbing that none of these faxes made sense.

"I'd better save the coffee break for when I get caught up," she admitted, and Rafe hesitated in the doorway.

"Take it easy, okay?" he cautioned her, evidently viewing the warning as even more vital than the coffee. "Give yourself time to get back on your feet."

Good advice, she knew, but that didn't make it any easier to ignore the pile of papers on her desk. She picked up the stack again, wincing at the thought of all those decisions to be made. "I just feel bad thinking about everyone in Chicago, waiting for me to get back—"

"Anne," he interrupted, crossing the room to pull the papers away from her and jamming them into a drawer. "Stop it. They're lucky to have you alive, period, and they can wait another couple months to have you back."

She should probably take offense at such high-handed behavior, but for some reason all she could feel right now was gratitude. Because this man, however dictatorial, was right. What mattered was being alive.

And everything else could wait.

"Thanks," she murmured, then saw the wreath of straw flowers in the drawer he'd left open. That Southwestern cluster of turquoise and coral blossoms mingled with twigs was part of the guest room decor, and its absence had puzzled her. "Oh, the desert wreath! I was wondering what happened to—"

But that didn't make sense, she realized with a sudden jolt of shock, and saw the same incredulity on Rafe's face before his expression grew softer.

"Beth must have told you a lot about the house," he observed.

That *did* make sense. Far more sense than feeling as if she and Beth had somehow traded places.

"That has to be why I know where everything goes," Anne agreed. And why she felt so very much at home here, as if she belonged in this house. It was the same sense of belonging she had felt when Rafe brought her Beth's clothes to wear home from the hospital—their luggage from the train was still lost somewhere—and she'd been overwhelmed with a sense of familiar comfort. "We must've spent so much time talking, it's like...well, kind of like she's still with me."

He regarded her curiously for a moment, but she saw no hint of doubt in his dark, watchful eyes. "Yeah?"

"I know that sounds weird, but—"

"No," he said gently, "not for twin sisters. And you two were pretty close. You talked every week."

They must have, because otherwise she couldn't possibly have known that Beth kept pencils in the file cabinet.

But how could she be so clear on pencils, on how to jiggle the bedside lamp switch, on the names of her sister's closest friends, and so vague on the details of her own life in Chicago?

"I wish I could remember more," Anne told him. "I know it'll all come back, but so far almost everything I remember is from when we were little."

"Give yourself time," he repeated, then sat down on the foot of the copper-varnished bed, facing her with a mingled look of resolve and entreaty. "Meanwhile, is there anything I can do?"

He'd done so much already that she hated to ask for more, but seeing her sister's wreath had reminded her of the need for a traditional farewell. She would never say goodbye to the memories of her twin, which seemed even stronger here in Beth's home, but after missing the funeral she needed to make some kind of gesture.

"Well, if you wouldn't mind…I'd really like to take Beth some flowers."

Rafe hesitated, and she saw his neck muscles tighten.

"It's okay," she said hastily. The man didn't need any more reminders of what he'd lost. "I can do that later."

"No." He stood up, squaring his shoulders. "No, you need to say goodbye." Then he glanced at his watch. "Let me just—"

"Rafe, not now!" Surely he didn't think she meant him to drop everything and escort her to the cemetery this very minute. "I just meant, when you get time."

But apparently he was already recovered from that

moment of hesitation, because he asked, "How about tomorrow?"

After more than two weeks since her sister's death, there couldn't be any rush about saying goodbye. And yet visiting Beth's grave might let her start working through the grief, accepting the loss and moving on.

"Well," she said softly, "if that's all right with you."

"Yeah, it's okay. It's fine." He walked back to the door, then turned to face her again, as if he needed to explain himself. "I haven't been there since the funeral."

"You don't have to—" she began, and he cut off her protest.

"No, I do. How about, I pick you up from your session with Cindy and we'll stop for flowers on the way."

Suddenly the man was sounding more like an attorney than she'd ever imagined him—more decisive and also more determined—yet somehow she had the impression that his take-charge demeanor was only a facade.

"Is that all right?" she faltered. "I don't want to put you through—"

"Anne, come on." Even his posture had changed; he was standing with an attitude of confidence that bordered on defiance. "I can handle it."

"Well, it's just…"

"I can handle it!"

"Because you're Mr. Tough Guy," she offered, and he responded with a startled expression.

"Did Beth tell you that?"

She must have. But anybody could see from his

stance, from the way he held himself ready for battle, that Rafe Montoya would stand alone against whatever challenge came his way—and that an offer of support would only make his determination more fierce.

"You don't need anyone looking out for you," Anne observed.

It surprised her when a flicker of remorse crossed his face. "No," he muttered, dropping his gaze to the carpet. "That drove her crazy."

And *that* sounded like the kind of marital problem a sister-in-law had better stay out of. "Look, I'm sorry," she said hastily, closing the drawer with the wreath, which had started her thinking of Beth. "This is none of my business."

He didn't even bother to voice an agreement. Instead, he straightened his shoulders as if dismissing the entire topic. "Anyway, let me know if you want some coffee later."

"Thanks." It actually sounded tempting, but she'd already intruded enough. "I ought to get some work done."

His smile flashed so quickly that she was caught by surprise at how attractive this man could be. "I hear you. The job comes first."

He was right, Anne thought a little breathlessly. What was the matter with her, anyway? Here she was, wearing her sister's clothes and living in her sister's home…but feeling her sister's appreciation for Rafe Montoya was going way too far.

"Tell me," she blurted, "how you and Beth met. I mean, the whole thing. How you fell in love with each other."

Rafe looked taken aback, but he shoved his hands into his pockets and leaned against the doorway, as if searching for the right words.

"Because you did love her," Anne prompted. "I mean, Beth probably told me the whole story at the time. It's just, I don't quite remember."

His guarded expression softened slightly. "Well," he said, "it was here in Tucson. You'd gone off to Harvard, and Beth was at the U of A."

"That was after our dad died, right?" She'd pieced together enough scraps of memory to know that their mother had died when they were young, and their late grandmother had raised them without much help from their dad. "So it was just Beth and me left."

"Right, and she came to this homeless shelter with a bunch of her sorority sisters. Volunteer weekend. I was coming off shift—this was an internship, my last year of school—and when I saw her reading to these kids, it just kind of hit me."

"Love at first sight," Anne said. This was what she needed, hearing about Beth from someone else who had loved her. And already the story was setting off chords of memory. "She'd never met anyone like you."

Rafe gave her a rueful smile. "She didn't know the half of it…I didn't want to scare her away. But I kept working extra hours, hoping I'd see her again, and she kept on showing up with dolls for the kids. You remember the dolls, right?"

"Nobody makes dolls who look like they have Down syndrome," Anne quoted her sister, who had spent years volunteering at the group home in their neighborhood. "And everybody should have a doll who looks like them."

"Of course you remember that," he apologized. "She wouldn't have turned it into a business without your marketing. Anyway, that was how we met."

"And fell in love."

"And fell in love, yeah." Rafe hesitated, then squared his shoulders, and for a moment she saw a grimace of pain cross his face before he resumed his look of calm control. Even so, his voice was a little unsteady when he muttered, "Thanks for asking. I needed to remember that."

Chapter Three

He had loved Beth.

He needed to remember that, Rafe knew.

He needed to hold on to whatever he could, if he was going to get through this cemetery visit.

"You don't have to drive me," Anne had told him early this morning, as if she might have seen some sign of the uneasiness that had haunted him all night. "I can always get a cab from the physical therapy clinic."

But that wasn't how Beth would want her sister cared for, he knew. And he needed to care for somebody.

Especially after how badly he'd failed his wife. Letting her think the street kids mattered more than she did, letting her leave on vacation without making the time to fix things…

''No, I'll take you,'' he'd told Anne, and now they were almost to the Fairlawn Memorial Park.

With a bouquet of yellow roses and a wildflower wreath on the seat between them.

''I really appreciate this,'' she said. ''I know you've got a lot of work backed up.''

He did, but this visit mattered more. Because Anne needed this trip.

''No problem,'' Rafe assured her, pulling into a parking space. ''It's been twelve days since the funeral, and I should've come before now.''

But she surprised him with a quick gesture, laying her hand on his arm as if to cut off the very thought. ''Not if it tears you up inside. Beth wouldn't want that.''

No, she wouldn't. Not Beth.

If this visit tore him up inside, though, it was no more than he deserved for letting her leave with things still uneasy between them.

And besides, he could handle it. As long as he had Anne to look after, there was no risk of breaking down.

Even so, accompanying her across the endless lawn to Beth's grave cost him more self-control than he'd anticipated. And Anne seemed to realize that he wasn't quite as strong as he'd hoped, because she made no attempt to engage him in conversation.

Without speaking, he placed his sheaf of yellow roses by the headstone and retreated to give her some time alone with Beth's memory. Yet after a few minutes of what looked like silent prayer, she turned to him without even wiping away the tears on her cheeks.

"Rafe," she said softly, "you have a right to feel bad, too."

"I know." But crying wasn't an option. He swallowed and shoved his hands into his pockets. "It's okay."

"I mean," she faltered, addressing the flowers in her hands as if meeting his gaze might be too intimate, "I know you feel like you have to look out for me, but if you need a shoulder to cry on…I can look out for you, too."

"That's okay," he said hastily. This trip was for Anne, not himself, but it was kind of her to make such an offer. "Thanks."

She seemed to realize that he didn't need comforting, because without another word she turned back to the grave and gently laid her own flowers next to his. Then she stayed still, probably saying goodbye to her sister in her own way, which Rafe hoped would take a while.

Because he needed to get himself back in control. Back to the kind of strength he'd relied on for years, the kind that kept him looking out for whoever needed protection.

Which didn't include Rafe Montoya.

No matter what Anne thought. But since she wouldn't be around for long, anyway, there was no point in explaining that he didn't need a shoulder to cry on.

Never had, never would.

So get yourself together.

It helped to remember the day of the funeral, Rafe discovered, mentally reviewing all the mourners he'd seen around the closed casket. Beth's friends from the quilt shop. The whole crew from Legalismo, because he hadn't thought to insist on keeping the clinic open. A couple of former clients. Their old neighbors from across the street, the Harts, Roger and Linda and Marci and Jim….

"Thanks for bringing me," Anne said, startling him with the realization that he'd completely lost track of the present. But apparently she had finished crying, leaving her wreath behind, because she was standing beside him and looking a lot more composed. As if she'd unloaded whatever grief was haunting her. "I needed to say goodbye."

"I'm glad it helped," he managed to answer as they started back toward the car. Back to real life, with its ongoing list of demands. Which reminded him of the guy who'd come in this morning, worried about his girlfriend taking their baby to Mexico. "Listen, if I go back to work tonight, will you be okay?"

She shot him a surprised glance. "Of course."

Maybe he was judging all women by Beth, who'd hated it when he stayed late at the clinic. "You sure? I don't want to leave you alone if you need—"

"A shoulder to cry on?"

He hadn't even thought of that, but of course he'd be there for her if she needed to cry. "Well, yeah," he said, reaching for his car keys. "Whatever I can do."

Anne waited until he'd opened her door before fixing him with a wry gaze. "Kind of a one-way street we've got here, isn't it?"

What, just because he wouldn't cry on *her* shoulder? "Look," he explained, holding his hands out in case she needed assistance, "I take care of people. I don't need people taking care of me."

She settled into her seat without taking his hand, moving so much more easily than yesterday that he felt a jolt of admiration for the physical therapist. "Ever?"

"Well, not since I was a kid." Not since his mother had fled the burden of caretaking. Not since he'd learned it was all his fault.

Anne reached for her seat belt, flinching a little as she stretched her arm back, and returned her gaze to his. "Tell me about when you were a kid."

Maybe she thought it would help him let go of some old grief or something, but he couldn't expect her to enjoy hearing about his childhood in the barrios of L.A.

"That's a story for some other time," Rafe said lightly, closing her door and moving to his own side of the car.

But as soon as he took his seat, Anne shifted her posture as if to get a better look at him. "All right," she said, and in her voice he heard the same determination he used to hear from Beth, whenever she tried to nurture him. "I'll make sure and ask some other time."

Some other time took a few days to arrive, but she wasn't going to let him out of talking about his life. Not when, Anne suspected, this man was carrying more grief than anyone should have to carry alone.

So when Rafe picked her up after her last therapy session of the week and apologized for having to return to the clinic as soon as he dropped her off, she told him to skip the trip home. "I'll just go with you," she said, and felt a shimmer of satisfaction when he turned the car around.

Maybe a visit to Legalismo would give her the chance to help Rafe Montoya.

Because there was something bothering him, she knew. And if she could encourage him to talk about it—not directly, not when he'd made it clear that he didn't need any nurturing—she might feel more capable of honoring Beth's wishes.

Her sister wanted the people she loved to be taken care of, and Rafe needed someone to talk to.

There wasn't much time for talk, though, she discovered when they arrived at the clinic and he introduced her to Oscar, a threatening-looking teenager who was evidently helping him replace a window.

"Only one bullet," Oscar told him, fingering a dent in the wall behind Rafe's desk. "Good aim, that's all."

Anne swallowed a gasp. "Somebody shot at you?"

"No, we were closed," Rafe said, rolling up his sleeves while Oscar removed a sheet of cardboard from the window frame. "This happened last night, I just never got time today."

He sounded as matter-of-fact as if the window had been shattered by a baseball, but apparently her start of alarm raised a red flag, because he turned to her with his usual swift offer of aid.

"Why don't I take you home and come back later? You don't need to wait around here."

"No, that's okay." If she waited, it would give her a chance to read the Legalismo flyers she'd seen on the battered coffee table. And that, in turn, might give her some clue to drawing out this man. "Really, I'm fine. You guys go ahead and fix things."

"This won't take long," Rafe promised as he and Oscar turned their attention to the pane of glass in the corner, so she returned to the lobby with its green plastic sofa and dented folding chairs. And by the time she made her way through the company-history brochure, halfway listening to the dialogue in Rafe's office, she found herself more intrigued than ever.

How did he *do* that? she wondered. How did a Law Review attorney, regardless of his past experience, keep up such a natural, easy conversation with a gang-tattooed boy who responded only in monosyllables?

How could Rafe do such a breathtaking job of caring for everyone around him, and refuse to accept any support for himself?

And why should she care?

But she did, Anne knew, even though she had never been much of a nurturer. That was Beth's role, while hers was to succeed in the world. Yet maybe the loss of her sister had made a difference in her priorities…because right now this man's welfare mattered far more than any business.

More than anything, she wanted to give him a chance to let down his guard.

"Thanks," she heard him tell Oscar, who came back through the lobby and headed outside without even a glance at her. All right, they must be finished—which meant she could start another attempt at looking out for the man her sister had loved.

"I didn't think lawyers could install windows,"

she told Rafe when he came down the hall, buttoning the cuffs of his sleeves.

"Depends on where they practice," he replied, then shot her a quick grin as he wiped a streak of plaster dust off his face. A simple gesture, but one which—without any warning—suddenly made her heart skip a beat. "We're in a pretty good location for this part of town, but bulletproof glass would be nice."

Anne caught her breath. She had no business reacting to the sight of this man—not even in the context of physical labor, which made her more aware of his powerful body—with such raw, primitive yearning.

"Is it safe," she asked, hoping her voice sounded normal, "working here?"

"Pretty much." He evidently hadn't noticed any flush of warmth on her skin, for which she could only be grateful, because he was moving with his usual unconscious grace. Opening the door, reversing a sign, twisting home the lock. "I won't let the interns work alone, but I've never had any problems."

She was supposed to be offering support, here, but for the moment all her carefully rehearsed openings had vanished, leaving her with a faster pulse and the desire to blurt out any question, any distraction she could think of. "Uh, do your clients carry guns?"

Rafe held up the No Drugs/No Weapons sign he'd just removed from the door and set it on the coffee table. "Not inside," he announced, then glanced back at his office. "I just need to grab a few things, and we're out of here."

"Take your time," she told him, and used the free

minute to steady her breathing, pressing her hands against her thighs until she felt herself edging back into common sense. Enough so that by the time he returned with a handful of file folders, she was able to ask a casual question.

"Was this a pretty typical day?"

"Well, it's not every day we have to replace a window." He gave her an apologetic smile as he turned toward the ancient answering machine on the front desk. "Sorry that took so long."

"No, I enjoyed seeing you in action." Which wasn't what she'd meant to say! Although she *had* enjoyed hearing his conversation, even before he came down the hall adjusting his shirt—and she'd better change the subject fast. "Is Oscar some kind of an assistant or something?"

Rafe picked up the machine and shook it until a red light came on. "I'm just keeping an eye on him."

"How come?"

"He reminds me of myself, I guess." He met her gaze with the same half confident, half defiant expression she'd noticed the other day, then set the machine back in place. "I'd like to see him get out of here."

So her impression of Oscar as the dangerous type had been valid, Anne realized. Because according to the company brochure, Rafe himself had grown up as a gang member in Los Angeles...until his last juvenile conviction had started him down the road toward rehab, law school and the crusade to help kids like those he'd done time with.

"I saw that fund-raising story about your background,'' she told him, and saw his posture stiffen as he headed down the hall.

"That was Peter's idea," he said, snapping off the light switch at the end of the hallway. "Guy who put up the money. He said we'd get a lot more donations if people saw a poster child make good."

Although his face was obscured by the shadows as he came back toward the lobby, she heard the thread of uneasiness in his voice. "How do you feel," Anne asked, "about being a poster child?"

He hesitated for a moment, then she saw his expression grow more determined, more resolute as he came into the light.

"It gets the job done."

And getting the job done, she suspected, was worth any amount of sacrifice. If he was ashamed of his past, the way she suspected from the sound of his voice, he wouldn't let that interfere with helping Legalismo.

"This really matters to you," she said softly, "doesn't it."

"Yeah." Rafe moved past her toward the desk, where he retrieved what looked like an appointment book from the center drawer and reached for a pencil. "I want to get some of these kids on track."

"Who did that for you?"

"Lot of people," he answered without looking up from the page. "I'm still paying it back."

Which would explain his passion for the job, and why Beth had complained that he put his crusade ahead of his marriage. But paying back implied a time limit, which she couldn't remember her sister mentioning. "For how long?"

He glanced at her then, checking off one last name on the page. "Beth always asked that, too."

Maybe because she'd recognized that Rafe was already doing more for the world than it had done for him. "And what did you tell her?"

Shutting the appointment book, he slid it back into the drawer and straightened up. "Long as I can do somebody some good," he said, reaching for his keys. "These kids—somebody's gotta be there for 'em."

It looked like he was getting ready to lock up, but she hated to leave right now. Not when a glimpse of his personality was almost within reach.

"Was anybody there for *you?*" she asked as he locked the desk drawer. And when he didn't answer, she offered a prompt. "Your parents?"

"My mom took off when I was three." He glanced around the room, as if making sure all the closing chores were complete. "My dad left me with a neighbor who left me with Aunt Nita, who left me with my grandfather, who—" Then he broke off, as if only now realizing what a narration he'd begun. "Long story. Anyway, you ready to go?"

No, although clearly his chores were finished. But they couldn't leave with his story hanging in limbo like that, because finally she might be near his motivation to avoid needing anyone. "How many people left you?" Anne blurted.

"What, you want a head count?" He sounded amused rather than annoyed, but he made no attempt to offer a count. "It was a long time ago."

All right, then. She wasn't going to push for whatever lay behind that nonchalant defense...at least not now. Instead, she reached for her purse, then caught her breath. Cindy had warned her not to sit still for more than five or ten minutes without shifting her posture, but she hadn't realized how much that warning mattered.

Because right now she couldn't stand up without Rafe's help.

Although helping her up probably wouldn't affect him one bit, since he'd been touching her with such casual courtesy all along. She just needed to forget that bizarre moment of longing, which had swept through her a few minutes ago, and focus instead on—

On—

Oh, the business. Legalismo.

"Rafe," she said hastily as he came toward her, "I should have told you this sooner, but I really admire what you're doing here."

"Ah. Thanks." He leaned down, offering her his hands for as solid a grip as she needed, and as she rose from her seat she saw more warmth in his gaze than she'd ever noticed before.

"I mean," she faltered, "you're really making a difference in the world."

Why that statement should affect him so strongly she wasn't quite certain, but she saw an unmistakable glow of pleasure in his eyes as she recovered her balance.

"That means a lot," he said, keeping hold of her hands until she felt the pulse of warmth between them swirling even higher, then quickly letting her go. "Thanks."

* * *

It shouldn't mean so much that somebody admired his work, Rafe told himself, handing his card to the judge's clerk. Anne was just being polite, same as all the well-meaning donors who raved about the importance of saving kids from gangs.

But somehow her acknowledgment, coming from a woman so much like the one who'd resented his passion for Legalismo, made him smile every time he remembered it.

Like now, while he was waiting for Diego's file, and mentally replaying this morning's conversation with the physical therapist.

"Anne is terrific," Cindy had told them both. "Lucky in the first place, yes, but also a really dedicated worker. And doing so well, she can start driving anytime now."

Which was great, since he'd had to work around her schedule no matter how often she insisted she could take a cab.

But in a way, he would miss the conversations they'd shared on the way to her morning sessions and on the way home at night—

"Here you go," the clerk told him, and he jerked his attention back to the judge's office.

"Thanks," Rafe muttered, and headed outside. His next mission was to check for messages, see if Anne was doing okay. See if she needed a ride home yet. She'd promised to call when she was ready to leave, but his cell phone had to stay silent in the judge's chambers.

It rang the moment he switched it back on, and he felt a flash of pleasure before realizing that such intense happiness didn't make sense. This might not even *be* Anne.

And even if it was, so what? The woman was his sister-in-law!

The caller, though, was the newest intern at Legalismo, Heidi, who had drawn front-desk duty for the day.

"I just thought you should know," she told him, "someone called about the train crash. They're returning Beth's luggage, so I told them to bring it here."

Real life couldn't have intervened at a better time, Rafe decided. He needed a reminder of Beth right now, before he found himself edging toward fantasies that were completely out of line.

"If you want," Heidi continued, "I can just put everything in the storage room until you're ready. Because I remember when my dad died, it took my mom a long time to go through his things."

That hadn't struck him as a problem, although he'd been living with Beth's things all along. He'd actually been seeing Beth's face and her body and her clothes on Anne every day, so seeing the clothes she'd taken to California shouldn't be any different.

"It's okay," he said, "I'll swing by on the way home. Did they mention finding Anne's things?"

"No, just Beth's. I don't think they're very well organized."

Anne might regret not having her own clothes back, although that would likely happen within the next few days. Meanwhile, there was no point in mentioning the find. He could go through Beth's luggage on his own.

But it surprised him that night, handling the clothes from his wife's severely battered suitcase, how much her scent resembled Anne's. Maybe that was always the case with twins, but somehow he'd never noticed the similarity between his wife's personal fragrance and her sister's.

Which was something he needed to forget.

Because thinking that way about Anne was completely unacceptable.

Rafe picked up another shirt, caught Anne's scent again and closed his eyes. He'd loved *Beth,* not her sister, so these feelings were way out of line. It would be one thing if he'd accidentally mistaken Anne for her twin—which people probably did all the time—but he knew perfectly well who was in the guest room down the hall.

And he couldn't let himself think about her.

He had to focus on his wife.

Finding Beth's silver earrings in the pouch made it easier, because he immediately flashed back to the first time they'd exchanged Christmas gifts. She had loved the earrings, put them on immediately, and insisted he open his instant camera right away so he could take a picture of her wearing "the best present ever."

They'd taken the camera with them on a picnic that afternoon, enjoying the winter sunshine that turned Sabino Canyon into a haven for hikers, and found a secluded clearing where their picnic had turned into a memorable celebration.

It would've been memorable even without the mesquite fiasco, but that had provided a note of drama when they wound up rolling off their blanket and into a low-branched tree...which left scrapes that neither of them noticed until much later. Rafe had used the last of their water to clean the gouge on her thigh, which left a faint scar that she called her "picnic souvenir," and it became one of his favorite places to kiss.

Because it always made her laugh. And then she'd pretend to tickle him, and he'd pretend to fight her off, and—

God, he missed her!

Beth was the woman he had loved, no question, and they'd shared some wonderful times. For nearly three years, he'd been closer to her than anyone he'd ever known, building a life together which exceeded his oldest dreams. Maybe it wasn't perfect, not with all the hours he worked, but even so their marriage had been the best relationship he'd ever shared.

The best of his life...

With a sigh he set her silver earrings on the dresser, then her bag of cosmetics, then rummaged in the side pocket of the suitcase and found only a few items left. A hotel postcard. A golf pencil. A crumpled flyer from the train dining car, where he knew she'd planned to share an end-of-vacation breakfast with Anne.

And on the back of the flyer, he saw Beth's writing.

It would be sweet if she'd started a letter to him and forgotten to mail it. Like finding an unexpected gift from his wife. Rafe smoothed out the paper and gazed at her handwriting, which formed an uneven headline on the page.

Pros & Cons of Staying Married/Getting Divorced. What?

He squinted at it again, trying to come up with some reason this was okay—like if she was helping a friend with a troubled marriage, or taking notes while watching a talk show. But already his eyes were betraying him, racing down the list of pros and cons, and he felt a hollow ache creeping through his bones.

Beth's life lay before him, and it looked like she hadn't wanted him there. Because...

Lonely.

The word was a condemnation, appearing at the top of each column. She might be lonely without him if they got divorced—but apparently she was just as lonely being married.

Rafe crumpled the paper in his fists, then jerked it open again. He'd failed her worse than he realized by insisting they could wait for a baby, failed her right here in black and white, and the least he could do was to read what he'd done. So he gritted his teeth and stared at the list.

Doesn't want a family.

Never home.

Never talk.

Doesn't care.

God, was that what she thought? She must have, because balanced against the considerations of "keep marriage vows" and "not sell the house," the reasons for divorce stood out far more clearly.

No baby.

No sharing.

No time.

But he had *tried,* damn it! He'd spent time with her, making a special point of it whenever things got too busy at the clinic. He'd set aside evenings for

dinner with Beth, worked at keeping the conversation
entertaining—none of the grim details that polluted
his days—and he would've sworn that she'd enjoyed
those nights as much as he did.

So how could she say there was no sharing? No
intimacy? He'd given Beth more of his heart and soul
than he'd ever given anyone, and it still—

It still wasn't enough.

And now it would never be enough.

Rafe threw the paper into the suitcase, then
slammed the lid shut. Yanked it off the bed and
hurled it onto the floor. Swore without even hearing
himself, kicked the suitcase under the bed, but it
wouldn't fit—damn it, *nothing* fit, nothing worked!—
so he jerked it up, cursing again—but now there was
something burning his throat, his lungs, not even his
voice was working right—and then he saw Anne hes-
itating at the door.

"Rafe," she asked, "are you all right?"

That was a stupid question, Anne realized as soon
as she asked it. Nobody swearing with such harsh
ferocity could possibly be all right. And he looked
awful, balanced on some sizzling edge between anger
and pain.

"No," he muttered, lifting a hand as if to warn her
from coming any closer. "Just—"

If he thought she would leave him this way, the
man didn't know her very well. Anne took a few steps
toward him, knowing she was safe in spite of his rage,
and wished she'd moved faster when she first heard
him slamming things.

"What's wrong?" she asked.

To her relief, he didn't even attempt a pretense that everything was fine. Instead he set down the suitcase he'd been kicking a moment ago, and she saw in his posture the raw anguish of defeat.

"She was leaving me," he blurted, yanking open the scorched lid and reaching inside for a crumpled piece of paper. "Beth. She didn't want to be married."

"Oh, no." She felt a sinking sensation in her chest, a mixture of sorrow and disbelief. It didn't seem possible Beth would leave him, not when it was obvious how much he'd loved her. Besides, anyone married to a man like Rafe Montoya— "No."

"I thought," he began, then faltered. "We had some problems, yeah. But I never thought—" He gestured with the letter, gripping it so tightly his hands looked white. "She wrote it all down."

What, a letter instead of a goodbye? "That doesn't sound like Beth," Anne protested as he returned the page to the suitcase with abrupt, almost jerky movements. "I can't believe she would've left you with just a note."

"No," he agreed with an edge of bitterness in his voice, "she would've told me in person. She wouldn't just…walk off." Then, as if the phrase had triggered some unbearable memory, he covered his face with his hands. "God."

Nobody should have to endure this kind of heartbreak, and yet she couldn't even think of how to comfort him. "Oh, Rafe."

"I never—" He drew a shuddering breath and looked up again, his eyes stark with devastation. "She never knew I loved her."

But that didn't seem possible, either. Anyone loved by this man would surely feel the passion in him. "She *must* have."

"Not well enough," he said bleakly. "I couldn't do it." Which didn't make sense—anyone could see he loved his wife, but already he was turning up his hands in an expression of futility. "I've never been any good at…at…"

She couldn't let him start running himself down, Anne thought. Not when he was already hurting so badly, and not when it was patently wrong. "You're good at a lot of things!"

"Not this." He sounded so certain that she caught her breath. And he must have seen her getting ready to protest, because he interrupted with a ragged explanation. "Not loving. She wanted more than I could give her, and I never even saw it."

"Rafe…"

"I can't do it!" he cried, and for a moment she heard his soul straining against its usual barrier. "I don't have the…the heart, the love, the—" Then he broke off, as if only now realizing how much he'd revealed to a virtual stranger, and closed his eyes for a moment. "God, I'm sorry. Don't let me dump all this on you."

He was ready to retreat behind his defiant self-confidence again, and Anne took a step closer to him. "I wish you would," she said gently.

"I just…" He drew a shaky breath, then stopped. Hesitated. Tried another breath, and she reached to draw him toward her.

"Rafe, you need to let yourself grieve."

With a shuddering gasp, he stumbled into her arms,

and she held him as close as she could. If he would just let go, just let himself cry....

"I can't," he choked.

"It's okay," she murmured in an effort at reassurance. For a man this strong to break down, he would have to feel incredibly desperate—and incredibly safe. But if only she could give him that safety.... "It's okay to hurt," Anne said softly. "It's okay to cry."

He buried his face against her shoulder, but she could still feel the resistance in him. "No—"

"It's okay," she repeated, and felt a searing compassion rising inside her. "Oh, Rafe…"

And then, as if something inside him had snapped, he let go a harsh breath—took another—held it for a brief, unsteady moment—and started to cry. Choking back sobs, struggling for breath, while she held him and whispered a litany of comfort. Of consolation, of tenderness, of all the reassurance and warmth and care she could offer. "Rafe, it's okay. Oh, Rafe…"

"I can't," he repeated, and she cradled him against her, stroking his hair, feeling his arms encircling her shoulders as if he needed all the support he could get. She would give it, gladly—and he must have sensed that here was the security he needed to let go, because finally he was abandoning any attempt at regaining control and letting himself give way to grief.

Raw, harsh grief. From a man who lived behind such solid strength that he'd probably never allowed it, never permitted the wall around his heart to crack. But now he was clinging to her with the same ferocity she'd glimpsed whenever he faced a challenge, holding her as desperately as a lifeline, and she held him with all her heart, anchoring his body, rubbing his back, smoothing his shoulders, bolstering his soul. Promising safety, promising warmth, promising whatever he needed to get through this torrent of grief and betrayal and loss.

He didn't deserve such loss! Nobody deserved pain like this, but all she could do was hold him, nurture him, protect him from hurt. Murmur sounds of support, whispers of encouragement, and let him cry in her arms. Shelter him against her, giving him refuge and comfort and warmth, because all he needed was someone to hold him, someone to be there....

And she would be there as long as he needed, as long as the sobs crashed through his body, shaking him, burning him—but already they were slowing, easing a little, letting him breathe. "It's okay," she whispered again, still stroking his hair, his back, still keeping him safe. Until, when he finally lifted his face to hers, she saw that he'd made it, he'd come through in one piece...and in a rush of affection, she gently touched his cheek.

Rafe pulled her closer to him.

Then drew a long breath, gazing at her in silence.

The silence held.

And the warmth began to build.

Shimmering between them.

Pulsing with a curious current of heat.

Rising.

Growing steadily stronger.

Flaring into—

Anne jerked away, and so did he. In the same moment, as if a crash of thunder had separated them. What on earth—?

"God," Rafe muttered, looking suddenly aghast. "Anne…"

She had to struggle for breath, had to look just past his eyes, because she couldn't let herself meet his gaze. Not now. Not yet.

"It's okay," she said hastily.

Knowing it wasn't.

"I didn't mean—" he blurted, and she hurried to interrupt him.

"No, of course not." Nobody could have meant for such a startling awareness to flash between them, nobody could have expected it to rise as swiftly as that. Holding him, rubbing his back, touching his face was supposed to be comfort, reassurance, not this throbbing awareness of heat. "Neither did I."

"I was…" he faltered, fumbling for an explanation. "I was just…"

"Upset, that's all." People did all kinds of crazy things when they were upset, right? So maybe they should treat this whole thing like an accident. Which of course it was, but still…! "We were both upset," she repeated, "talking about Beth. But, listen, I didn't mean to—"

"No, I know," he said quickly. "It's all right."

Yet this man was her sister's husband, so how *could* it be all right? Comfort was one thing, but for that sizzling moment she hadn't even been thinking of comfort.

And neither had he.

Which meant, she realized with a tremor of dismay, they couldn't very well pretend things were the same as ever. Besides, no matter how innocently she'd intended to honor Beth's wishes, this whole incident was her fault. She had been living in the man's house, enjoying his company, encouraging him to give way to his feelings, and now— "I'll move into a hotel."

"Anne, you don't need to do that." He looked hurt, although she couldn't imagine why. But when he muttered in a low voice, "It's not going to happen again," she realized that Rafe must think she no longer trusted him.

He must be blaming himself.

Same as she was blaming *her*self.

"Of course it's not," she agreed. Of course this would never happen again, because they would both make a point of staying on guard. "But things might be…awkward."

"No, listen, it's okay." He shoved his hands into his pockets and faced her directly. "We both know this was an accident."

"An accident." Maybe if they kept it in that context, rather than admitting any flash of desire, everything would settle down more quickly. "Right."

"So there's nothing to worry about," Rafe concluded, and the determination in his voice reassured her. He sounded so confident that Anne felt a flicker of relief.

Maybe they *were* back to normal.

A dedicated career woman, and a gangbanger-turned-counselor who'd happened to marry her sister.

"Right," she confirmed, forcing herself to meet his gaze and hold it…hold it…hold it, with her emotions pushed firmly out of the way. She could do this, Anne resolved. If he could watch *her* with no sign of uneasiness, no sign of turmoil, she could certainly do the same.

She could. She would.

"Right," she repeated, and let herself start breathing again. "Okay, then. There's nothing to worry about."

Chapter Four

There was nothing to worry about, Rafe reminded himself as he drove to work the next day without Anne, who had taken Beth's car this morning and pronounced herself perfectly safe driving alone.

There was nothing to worry about, he vowed again as he pulled into the parking lot outside the legal clinic.

They were both honorable people, and neither of them wanted to betray Beth's memory.

"Lawyer must've had a long night," Oscar greeted him, and Rafe felt his muscles tensing before he realized the kid was referring to the hour.

"Late start this morning," he admitted, unlocking the clinic door and trying not to think of Anne.

After all, it was out of respect for Beth that they'd come together in the first place.

Because they both knew she wanted her loved ones taken care of.

"So Cholo says he wants to meet you," Oscar announced, and Rafe forced his attention to the prospect of winning the Lobos gang leader's confidence.

"Anytime he wants to come by, I'll be here."

Legalismo or not, though, he was going to keep taking care of his sister-in-law. Not only for Beth's sake, but because he owed Anne…especially after she'd let him cry on her shoulder last night. She hadn't needed to do that, but she had been there for him wholeheartedly.

And that caring, that nurturance had been achingly sweet….

But of course it wasn't like he needed her, he reminded himself again during the lonely drive home after work. Even though he enjoyed the freedom to share clinic stories with someone who'd be gone in another month, there was no chance of him coming to need her in his life. Not when she'd be back in Chicago four weeks from now.

No danger at all.

And he was prepared for the impact of seeing her already inside the house, which was a good thing—because otherwise it would have startled him to walk in the kitchen door and find the table set, a tantalizing aroma of food he hadn't cooked, and a woman who looked like Beth taking a casserole out of the oven.

"You didn't have to do that," he protested, depositing his case files at the end of the counter before washing his hands at the sink. Beth had given up on timing dinner to coincide with his arrival, but it was always a nice surprise when it happened. "I was going to order pizza."

"Well, you've got a whole freezer full of food." Which was true, because her friends and the neighbors had showered him with donations lately. "I know Beth was a really great cook, and I didn't want to take over her kitchen—I mean, *your* kitchen—but anyone can heat up a casserole."

She'd done more than that, though, Rafe saw, glancing at the table with its glass bowl of salad, basket of crusty bread and pitcher of iced tea as she set the casserole dish by her place.

"That was really nice of you," he told her, waiting for her to sit down before taking his own seat. "But don't feel like you have to put in a whole day with Cindy and the business, and then start cooking."

Anne picked up the serving spoon and reached for his plate, already shaking her head.

"Look, you've done so much for me the past couple weeks...you *have* to let me help somehow."

If she wanted to do something for him, heating up a casserole was probably better than anything else he might think of.

"All right," Rafe said hastily, turning his attention toward the bread basket. "Thanks."

This was so much like the dinners he'd enjoyed with Beth that over the next half hour he found himself lapsing into the same shorthand he'd used with his wife, mentioning people without even stopping to wonder whether Anne might know them.

And she did a remarkable job of keeping up her end of the conversation. Either she was too polite to remind him that she'd never met the landlord of their first apartment, or Beth had shared far more stories than he realized.

But she didn't seem to mind his assumptions, and he was equally intrigued by her description of the day. Especially when she mentioned finding some half-finished doll designs in Beth's car, and wondering whether he'd mind if she tried to finish them.

"You should do it," Rafe assured her. It might be awkward if she tried to take over for Beth at home, but taking over her part of Dolls-Like-Me was only natural. "She'd want you to finish her work."

Anne hesitated a moment, watching him, then picked up their empty plates and went to the sink. Almost as if she wanted to put some distance between them.

"Okay, then," she agreed, turning on the faucet. "I just don't want to be...well, presumptuous...about anything."

"No, look, it's your company, too. I guess now, actually, the whole thing is yours." He hadn't even thought about what to do with Beth's ownership, but returning it to Anne made the most sense. Rafe swallowed the last of his iced tea and deposited both their glasses in the dishwasher. "We'll need to go over all that, one of these days."

"Later, all right?" She looked slightly uncomfortable as she turned off the water and brought their plates to the bottom rack. "There's no rush, and I'm still not caught up with everything."

Rafe set to work clearing the rest of the dishes from the table, letting Anne take care of the casserole dish. "Cindy said you're doing great."

"Maybe with the exercises. But it's a lot harder

than I expected, understanding all the reports from Chicago.''

There were still some pretty big gaps in her memory, but Dr. Sibley had repeatedly explained that the effect of traumatic injuries could be hard to predict. Still, with her physical recovery progressing so rapidly, her memory shouldn't be too far behind.

And when that happened, maybe she could offer him some insights.

Because if Beth had written that pro-and-con list during their train trip, surely she would've talked about it with her sister.

"You'll probably start remembering soon," he offered, and Anne nodded as she scooped the leftovers into a plastic container.

"I know. Sometimes I get these quick little glimpses of the office and my apartment, but the clearest memories are all from when we were little."

Had she ever noticed, he wondered, that she spoke of her childhood as a plural experience?

"Like watching a movie," she continued, heading for the refrigerator, "only I'm living it. I can still see us on the couch with Grandma, how she'd read us stories on her lap...."

He could picture them together, and it was a charming vision. "I bet you were cute back then," Rafe observed, remembering Beth's description of their matching pigtails. "I wish I'd known you."

It wasn't until her step faltered that he realized that such a statement might be a little too personal. Time for a fast change of subject. Anything. Childhood. "So, did you have any pets?"

That was pretty lame, but she accepted the diversion readily. "Just goldfish," Anne replied. Closing the refrigerator door, she turned back to him with an embarrassed grin. "We called them Windsong and Starfire."

He couldn't help smiling at the idea of twin sisters christening their goldfish. "Great names."

"Well," she explained, returning to the sink while he disposed of the bread, "we really wanted a horse."

Which must have been as unlikely a dream as the one he had cherished at that age. "I wanted a Porsche," Rafe admitted.

She turned on the water and nodded in commiseration. "I know."

He couldn't even remember mentioning that fantasy to Beth, but she must have shared it with her sister. And the fact that Anne would remember something so trivial was curiously satisfying—except he was *not* thinking that way.

"So," he said hastily, "neither one of us got what we wanted." Then realized that, once again, there was a statement better left unsaid. "I mean—"

"No," Anne interrupted, as if she too had recognized the danger of discussing unsatisfied wants, "I *did* get what I wanted. I have a great business in Chicago. I have a company to run."

Right, she did. And she didn't especially want or need a man in her life, Beth had always said, because she was devoted to her career.

"Yeah," he agreed, crumpling the paper napkin that lined the empty breadbasket and firing it into the trash. "You sure do."

"I'll be back there in another month," she continued doggedly, and he felt an aching tug of loss at the thought.

Oh, hell.

"Listen," Rafe blurted, "I need to finish up some work at the clinic." It was nothing that couldn't wait until tomorrow, but cleaning up the kitchen with Anne was a virtual minefield. Better to get out now, before this got any worse.

She seemed to recognize the same necessity he did, because he could see a rush of relief on her face as she reached for the soap bottle above the sink.

"That's fine," she told him. "Stay as late as you need to."

Obviously she didn't share Beth's attitude about him belonging at home in the evenings...which was just as well. And she'd said all along that she'd be okay on her own, but even so he felt obliged to make sure. "You don't mind being alone?"

"No, go ahead," Anne insisted, aiming a squirt of soap under the faucet. "The kids need you more than I do."

Which was true. Kids like Oscar and Paul and Vicente were far more likely to show up at night than they were during the day, and if he worked in the lobby he could meet whoever dropped by without the usual interference of eager-beaver interns.

"Actually," Rafe explained, "I've been thinking about staying open in the evenings." He'd thought of it last month and decided the hours were beyond his grasp, but now he had more incentive to stay away from home. "Make it a regular thing. Because some of the kids need a place to be, after hours."

"That's a great idea," she agreed, and he felt a

pleasurable rush of pride at how quickly she grasped the value of such a service.

And then a tremor of regret.

Which was completely inappropriate.

"Okay," Rafe said hurriedly, picking up his case files from the end of the counter and reaching for his car keys. "I'd better go now."

"Yes," Anne murmured, and as he turned toward the door he saw on her face the same dismay he'd seen whenever he left Beth alone at night. "You'd better go."

He'd left just in time, Anne told herself as she finished cleaning the kitchen and retreated to her room. Why hadn't she realized how hard it would be, sharing the kind of home-cooked meal Beth must have prepared every night?

And why hadn't she realized the danger of falling into her sister's identity?

She'd been *feeling* like Beth tonight, the entire time she used her sister's cookware and wore her clothes and chatted with her husband.

"Stop that!" she ordered herself aloud, but it didn't seem to help.

She gave herself the order again while using Beth's vanilla shampoo, which she liked so much she'd probably buy the same kind in Chicago.

And again while waiting for the sound of Rafe's car arriving home, at which point she immediately turned off her bedside lamp and tried to think about sleep.

But after a restless night, she knew she needed to set things straight. So she made a point of getting up early, in time to meet Rafe in the kitchen just before he left.

"Don't feel like you need to be home for dinner tonight," she told him. "I don't mean you *have* to work late or anything, but keeping the clinic open is a good thing."

He looked at her strangely as he picked up his car keys.

"I mean it," she said, easing away from his path toward the back door. "You've been wonderful about driving me wherever I have to go, but now I'm doing fine. So don't feel like you have to be here for me."

"Okay," Rafe said. "And don't feel like you have to cook for me—it was great, but it's not your job."

She was going to cook for herself anyway, but there was no point in arguing about it. "Sure," she agreed. "Anyway, stay as late as you need to."

He hesitated at the threshold, then shook his head in amazement. "Hearing you say that, it's...strange, that's all. Beth hated it when I didn't come home."

"Well, she was your wife," Anne reminded him before he headed outside. A wife had every right to make such demands, but not a sister-in-law. Not a house guest. Not a woman with a life of her own, back in Chicago.

A life she couldn't wait to get back to.

If only she could remember more about it.

"You'll remember," Cindy assured her that afternoon during their back exercises. "I've worked with people before who had this same kind of problem, with their memory knocked out of whack. Once they got back home, everything fell into place."

That would happen to her, too, surely. Already she

was recognizing the business manager's voice on the phone, and the orders he talked about each morning were beginning to sound more familiar.

"I know," Anne agreed, trying to flatten her shoulders against the table and gritting her teeth against the familiar pain. "I just wish I could make it happen sooner."

"Tired of me pushing you, huh?" Cindy grinned, adjusting the support pillow under her neck. "But any therapist you get is gonna make you do these lifts. It'd be the same in Chicago."

In Chicago, though, she would be where she belonged. Living her own life, instead of clinging to Beth's.

Which felt oddly comfortable, considering that she'd always been the career woman in their family. Rafe had told her how, after returning with an MBA from Harvard, she'd spotted the potential in her sister's doll-making venture. "Beth was just selling a few here and there," he'd explained, "and a year later you had locations all over the country. She always said nobody could do business better than you."

All the more reason, Anne decided the next morning as she set out his oatmeal and coffee—a practice that Rafe seemed to appreciate, even though he probably hadn't yet realized she was still cooking for them both—that she had to get back to Chicago soon. She had to resume her own life and stop driving Beth's car, using Beth's dishes, enjoying Beth's shampoo.

She had to stop noticing Beth's husband.

She had to call her office, and…and start concentrating on real life.

Henry, the Dolls-Like-Me manager, sounded delighted to hear from her when she reached him shortly before closing. "It'll be great having you back, as soon as you're ready. Your assistant's doing okay, but she doesn't know the business like you do. Any chance you'll be back next month?"

"Yes, I will. I promise." She couldn't very well ask Henry what kind of person she'd been outside of work, but why couldn't she remember any friends? All of Beth's friends had called to offer their sympathy, but surely she'd had time for some of her own. "Is there any, uh, personal mail waiting?"

He forwarded her to a secretary named Tina, whom she couldn't visualize, but who told her that only yesterday her new journal had arrived from Leatherworks. "Remember, you were upset when it hadn't come before you left? They finally sent it."

A journal? Maybe she had enjoyed keeping a diary, although that didn't sound familiar, either. But it might be the kind of habit which would only take a few minutes to resume.

"Just send it out here whenever you get time," she said, "but there's no rush." After all, a legal pad could serve as well as a leather-bound journal. "Thanks, Tina."

A diary. That might be what she needed to restore her sense of balance, of knowing her place in the world. Cindy, Dr. Sibley and everyone else had warned that it would take a while to truly feel like herself again…but this business of feeling like her sister was wrong.

Just wrong.

So that evening, relieved that Rafe was staying late at the clinic again, she made a solitary dinner, left his covered plate in the refrigerator, and then settled down at the kitchen table with a legal pad and pencil from Beth's file cabinet.

Where to start?

The date, maybe. It didn't look especially satisfying, but you had to start somewhere.

People talked to their journals, right? Like writing a letter. Somehow she suspected she wasn't much of a letter writer, not when a phone call would work just as well. But she wrote "Dear Diary" at the top of the page, then sat back and looked at it.

This wasn't going so well.

She didn't want to write, she wanted to *talk.* Talking to people made more sense than writing letters, or writing journals. Talking was more real, more fulfilling, because you were actively involved with someone else.

But the only person she could clearly remember talking to, often and intensely, was her sister.

And Beth was gone.

This was stupid! Anne decided, ripping off the top page of the legal pad. Writing didn't work. Unless maybe she could write to Beth...

"Dear Beth," she tried. "I miss you."

"I know."

She could almost hear her sister's voice, which sounded strangely like her own. But the response made sense, made her feel the same easy comfort she remembered from their phone conversations. So she started writing faster.

"I hate not having you here. It's like part of me is missing. Nobody will ever understand what it's like, not having you to talk to."

"I know."

"Even if we didn't talk every day, I always knew you were there. Now there's nobody left—Mom, Dad, Grandma—it was always just you and me, and now it's just me."

She was starting to cry, Anne realized, but there was something fiercely primal about talking to her sister. Maybe this wasn't as good as a phone call, but she had to talk to someone!

"I hate being alone," she wrote as the first tear dropped onto the page. "I act like I can handle it, but inside I'm so scared. And I know you're with me in spirit, but it's not the same thing."

"I know."

Of course Beth knew. They had known everything that mattered to each other, and—

Oh, dear God.

If Beth knew, there was no point keeping quiet about Rafe.

But how could she explain that flash of heat in his room the other night? It didn't make any sense, and if she couldn't understand it, how could Beth?

They couldn't talk about this. Not until she figured it out for herself. Anne ripped the page off the tablet, then blurted the truth to her sister.

"You know what's really awful? I feel like I'm taking over your life."

"It's your life, now."

Maybe in some cosmic sense, but that almost sounded as if she'd wished for a home in Tucson with vanilla shampoo and Rafe Montoya. "It's not supposed to be!" she protested, choking back another rush of tears. "I don't belong here. I don't want to take over your house, and your clothes, and your part of the company.''

''You are, though.''

She was, yes.

And what had it cost?

Her sister's life.

"It's not mine," Anne choked. "It's yours, and I can't take any of this away from you." No matter how much she might want it. "I never meant to— Beth, I didn't want you to die!"

The sob spilled over, and all she heard from her sister was silence.

"I didn't," she pleaded. "I swear, I didn't."

Still no answer.

"I wanted there to be two of us, forever and ever." They had sworn that together, linking their pinky fingers, back in third grade when Anne had brought home a library book about the oath of Cherokee blood brothers. "Remember?"

Maybe she was crying too loud, maybe if she stayed quiet she could hear her sister's voice. But somehow she couldn't stop crying, and she couldn't bear to think what Beth would say if she *could* hear her. Didn't her sister understand?

"I miss you," Anne told her, and felt the sobs coming even faster. "Beth, I miss you so much."

''I know.''

Oh, yes. Her sister's voice. Yes.

"It's like nothing is the same anymore," she blurted. "You're the only person who knows what it's like, and we can't talk like we used to!"

''I know.''

At least Beth was answering again. At least they

still shared some connection, however fragile. "And you know I wouldn't try and take over your life, don't you? I really, really don't want to do that."

Silence.

"Really," she repeated, but it didn't seem to make any difference. Because no matter how hard she listened, there was no response.

Beth was gone.

Again.

Still.

"I miss you," she whispered. This wasn't right, she had to make things right with her sister, and yet how could she possibly do that? There was nobody to talk to, nobody left, and no matter how hard she tried to stop crying, the tears seemed to have taken over her entire body and soul. Flooding, streaming, filling the kitchen with the sound of grief, harsh and aching and raw, but it didn't matter because no one could hear her anyway.

Nobody would ever hear, because her sister was gone.

She was alone.

And nothing would ever be all right again.

All right, Rafe decided as he parked his car beside Beth's and saw the kitchen lights on. Anne was still awake, but this didn't have to be difficult. All he had to do was say hello and good night. Head straight for bed and take the files with him rather than discussing his work in the kitchen.

He could get through this just fine.

Except that Anne was sitting at the kitchen table,

huddled over with her face buried in her hands, and sobbing as though her heart had broken.

"Anne?"

She jerked upright and stared at him, then made a futile attempt at looking normal.

"I'm sorry," she choked, although she had nothing to apologize for. "I was just talking to Beth, and—"

Was that what had her so upset?

And what did she mean, talking to Beth?

"I mean, writing," she stammered, and he saw a legal pad with tearstains on the top page. "Instead of journaling. I was writing to her."

Anne was devoted to her journal, he remembered Beth saying. Beth hadn't been much for writing, but it made sense that her sister would seek solace in words on paper. "Ah."

"Like we used to talk, only I was imagining what she'd say, and—" She broke off, looking at the crumpled page on the table, then met his gaze with a troubled expression. "Rafe, I can't do this. I can't stay here."

He'd thought the same thing the other night, but keeping Legalismo open late ought to make things better.

"Sure, you can," he began, but she burst out with an explanation he had never anticipated.

"It's like I'm taking over my sister's life! And it's not my life."

Of course it wasn't, but that was no reason to leave Tucson with four weeks of therapy still left.

Besides, she had nothing to feel guilty about.

"You never wanted Beth's life," Rafe reminded her. "She always said you were the brains of the family—she was the heart—and each of you wound up exactly where you belonged.''

''That means I belong in Chicago,'' Anne said, and as she stood up he saw that her face was streaked with tears. ''I don't belong here.''

''Not for good, no.'' He knew that perfectly well, and he wished it didn't bother him. But there was no time for wishes, not while she was so upset. Not while she looked ready to bolt for the door. ''Even so, I'm not letting you leave like this.''

''You don't have to,'' she told him, and turned toward the phone. ''I'm calling a cab.''

This was happening too fast, and he couldn't let her walk out like this. ''Anne, wait a minute!'' he protested, moving swiftly to block her route to the phone. ''You're in no shape to be—''

''I'm trying to take over Beth's life,'' she interrupted fiercely, ''and it's *her* life. I have to get back to Chicago.''

''All right, yes.'' Eventually she would have to get back, and there was no point wishing she could stay here forever. ''But do you think Beth would want you all alone in Chicago right now? Feeling like this?''

There was a silence.

''Do you?''

''No,'' she whispered.

''No,'' he agreed through a rush of relief, and felt the tension in his body start to ease. ''She wouldn't.'' And neither did he want Anne alone in Chicago, feeling this upset. ''Not now.''

But by the time she finished with her therapy, surely she'd be her usual self again. He'd be *his* usual self again, and they could say goodbye with the same courtesy they'd always shown as in-laws.

Nothing more.

"I'll go tomorrow," she said, and he felt his muscles tighten. This battle wasn't nearly finished.

"Anne, look," Rafe told her, taking a seat at the table in hopes that she'd sit down across from him. Away from the phone. "I know what you're going through."

"No, you don't." She sat down, but she still didn't look comfortable. "You're not betraying your sister—"

"Neither are you!" he interrupted, but she didn't even seem to hear him. Instead she ran her hands across her face, as if trying to clear the last trace of tears away, and met his gaze again.

"I'm taking over her life," she said quietly. "And that's wrong."

Of course that would be wrong, but she wasn't taking over Beth's life. "You're finishing her designs, that's all."

Anne shook her head. "I'm wanting her job, I'm *loving* her job, I'm wanting her house and her clothes and her—" Then she broke off, as if that sentence was too damning to finish, and concluded instead, "I'm living with her husband."

So.

So she was feeling the same desire he was.

But they both knew it was completely inappropriate, and they were both rational adults.

"Nothing's happened," Rafe reminded her. Which wasn't enough of an assurance, he knew, but for some reason it was getting harder to maintain the emotional detachment he'd relied on since the train wreck. Still, he already knew he could do whatever he had to. "Nothing *will* happen. Anne, I give you my word."

That didn't seem to comfort her the way a promise should, because she still looked uneasy. "You don't think…" she began, then faltered.

"I think," he said carefully, "the past few days, we've both been upset." That was true enough, and he had to use whatever he could to keep her from walking out in such sorry shape. He had to do a better job of making her feel safe. "But we both loved Beth. Right?"

"Right."

All right, stay focused on the important part. Forget about how she made him feel. "And we both know Beth would want you to stay here," he continued. "Right?"

"Oh…she would, I know." Anne hesitated, still looking distressed. "It's just—"

He had to give her something to hold on to, Rafe knew. Give them both a promise of security. "You'll be done with physical therapy in less than a month," he reminded her, and she gave him the same wry smile he had always loved on Beth.

"You think," she asked, "we can get through four more weeks?"

He felt his heart twist at the realization that this would be as tough for her as it would for him. But no matter how late he had to stay at the clinic, he couldn't forget why he'd invited her home in the first place.

"Beth would want you here," he said, and saw Anne close her eyes for a moment. She knew it the same as he did, and that knowledge would get them through the next few weeks of looking out for one another. Of looking just past one another. "So you've got to stay here, and we'll make this be all right."

She nodded slowly, then met his gaze again.

"All right. Four more weeks."

"Until Cindy says you're ready to go." If it took longer than four weeks, he'd deal with that later. He could do whatever he had to. "Then I'll take you to the airport myself."

Her smile flickered for a moment. "I'll plan on that."

He didn't want to think about saying goodbye at the airport, Rafe realized, which was disturbing enough to make him dismiss the thought altogether.

After all, it wasn't like he needed her to confide in. To make him feel wanted. To look for in the window whenever he returned home.

But for only four weeks, where was the harm?

"Okay," he said hastily, and stood up. "I'm gonna lock up for the night, and I'll see you in the morning."

She evidently recognized the wisdom of heading off in different directions, because she picked up her writing materials and started toward the hall. "Good night, Rafe. Good dreams."

"Good dreams…"

He stared after her, startled at hearing Beth's goodnight wish from a woman with the same voice, the same walk, the same smile. Of course it shouldn't surprise him, they were identical twins and they'd probably grown up hearing that same wish every night.

But even so, for a moment he found himself wondering if maybe somehow Beth had magically taken Anne's place.

Which was crazy, Rafe knew.

He was grasping at straws.

And the reason was humiliating, he admitted as he checked the door and turned off the kitchen lights. Rafe Montoya wasn't the kind of man who'd go lusting after his wife's sister, so of course the woman had to be his wife.

Forget it, Rafe ordered himself as he headed down the hall to his room, where he'd come so close to kissing her the other night. Wishing things were different was a waste of time, and he should have learned that by now.

But what if there'd been some mistake?

It was a fantasy, he knew. Look at how readily she'd accepted his decision to work late.

Beth wouldn't do that.

But look at how sweetly she'd tried to take care of him.

Beth *would* do that.

Not that he needed it. Not that he wanted it.

But what if there'd been some mistake?

Chapter Five

There was no mistaking the warmth between them. No mistaking the hardness of his body against hers. The way she arched her hips to meet him, the way—

No!

Anne sat up in bed, flooded with heat, feeling her heart racing far too fast. This was the second time tonight she'd dreamed of Rafe, and she had to make these dreams stop.

But the sensation had been so vivid, almost as if she were actually there in his bed. Because it was definitely his bed in the dream, with the light from the high window behind them. With the soft feel of his cotton sheets beneath her skin, the solid warmth of his chest, the coaxing pressure of his lips—

No, stop.

She wasn't remembering that.

It wasn't even her own memory, Anne reminded herself, turning on the bedside light to chase away any vestiges of sleep. Better to stay awake all night than to start that dream again. It was fantasy, it had to be, because surely her sister wouldn't have described the way Rafe felt in bed.

Beth would never have gone into such incredible detail about her husband's skin and his scent and the way his muscles clenched under her touch....

Which meant she was making up images out of nowhere, and those images went far beyond anything she had a right to imagine.

She had to stop.

Staying awake for the rest of the night would definitely do the trick. It might be stupid, neglecting her sleep—already she could hear Cindy warning her about the importance of rest—but tomorrow night things would be different. Because tomorrow she was going to spend the entire day remembering all the differences between Beth and herself.

Recovering her own memories, her own desires, her own dreams.

And setting aside her sister's.

With that resolved, she managed to fall asleep for another few hours, but still woke in time to hear Rafe's shower in the other bathroom. Better to stay in bed, Anne decided, than to get up and start the coffee, squeeze the orange juice, continue the breakfast-making habit which had felt so comfortable over the past few days.

Better to stay out of his way.

Except that wasn't really fair to Rafe.

After all, none of this was *his* fault. He didn't de-

serve to start another long day of clinic work without
so much as a good-morning cup of coffee.

And as long as she was making coffee, it was only
sensible to soft-boil some eggs, set out the crackers,
remember that he liked his toast as plain as his coffee.
It was the kind of gesture she'd offer anyone who
invited her for a visit. It didn't mean anything but
good manners.

But Rafe seemed more touched by the gesture than
she'd expected. "Anne," he said, "this is really nice
of you. I'd tell you to stop, but—"

"But I wouldn't," she interrupted. "We both need
a good start, because I have a lot to get done today…and you always do."

He smiled in acknowledgment. "I'm gonna meet
Cholo this afternoon. If everything goes well, it could
be a long night."

"This is one of the gang leaders, right?" From his
hesitant descriptions of clinic business, which she suspected might flow more freely now that they'd established her departure date, she knew how much this
could mean to Legalismo. "The one who might let
you work with his people?"

"If everything goes well," he repeated, and she
saw him touch the pocket where he kept a blessed
medal. A gift from his aunt, Rafe had said, looking
almost embarrassed at the idea of a talisman—but
he'd been carrying it ever since Legalismo started
staying open at night.

"And having this guy in your office is safe?"

"Yeah." Then, as if recognizing he might have
stretched the truth a little, he offered an amendment.

"Pretty much. You're not planning to come visit, are you?"

She hadn't even thought of it. "No," Anne assured him. "I've got plans already."

She did, a lengthy list that she'd started in her mind after vowing to clarify the differences between Beth and herself, and it would take most of the day. So after her two hours with Cindy and her review of the daily faxes from Chicago, she squared her shoulders and began the process of separating her sister's life from her own.

No more wearing Beth's clothes. She spent the afternoon at the nearest mall and came home with enough casual wear and toiletries to last her the rest of her visit.

No more of Beth's vanilla shampoo. With a new green-apple blend now in her shower rack, she resolutely returned the half-empty bottle to the cabinet under the sink.

Even that hair clasp wasn't hers to wear, Anne remembered when she glanced at the bathroom counter. Rafe had told her to take whatever she needed from her sister's dresser, the very first day she arrived, but the new comb would keep her hair off her face just as well as Beth's silver barrette.

All right, the barrette and the clothes had to go back in the master bedroom. It took only a few minutes to hang up the skirts, jeans and tops in their proper places, to return the shoes to the right location, and to remember where the jewelry belonged.

But when she opened the narrow drawer that contained Beth's jewelry box, she felt her heart lurch.

"He doesn't love me."

That didn't make sense, Anne knew. Of *course* Rafe didn't love her. But the feeling of despair that swept through her at the sight of the jewelry box felt so raw, so anguished that she had to brace herself against the dresser for a moment.

"He doesn't care."

This was Beth's grief, she realized. Beth's cry of desperation. And without knowing why, she lifted the top tray of the jewelry box and found a wedding ring lying alone.

Her sister's ring.

"I might as well not even be married to him."

The way he acts, like he doesn't need me at all, this ring doesn't mean anything!

Our marriage is practically over.

So try setting the ring aside.

Just go for a week without it, without this symbol of a marriage falling apart—

Anne caught her breath.

It was so clear, Beth's decision to leave the ring here, that she could almost feel her sister's anger, her frustration, her desperate awareness that Rafe cared far more about the Legalismo kids than a family of his own.

"I know we said we'd wait for a family, but the clinic is taking forever!"

Oh, Beth.

"It's not fair. I thought a baby would bring us closer together, but I'm always going to come second."

But Rafe...

"He doesn't love me."

Oh, this hurt.

This hurt more than the back exercises, more than the knowledge of being alone. It was Beth's hurt, Anne knew, but even so it felt painfully close to her own. She could feel all too fully the despair with which her sister had set aside this wedding ring.

The blind, unreasoning hope of pretending the marriage had never happened.

The yearning for a closeness that Rafe would never, ever allow.

It was her sister's grief, not her own, but even so she could feel it in her bones and in her blood. And though there was nothing she could do about it, she wished with fierce desperation that she could make things better.

Wished she could open Rafe's heart.

Wished he could *see* how much he was loved....

"Anne?"

His voice, calling from the kitchen, startled her. What was he doing home at three in the afternoon? Anne slammed the jewelry box shut, dropped the barrette into the drawer and closed it with a quick shove, then glanced in the dresser mirror.

She didn't know what to tell him yet, but would he see any sign of turmoil?

No, she decided, maybe her eyes were a little darker than usual, but he probably wouldn't notice a thing. Which, until she figured out whether or not to mention Beth's hurt, was probably just as well.

"Just putting away some shopping!" she called back, and started down the hall with as calm an expression as she could manage. Without any idea of how to explain it, of how Rafe could deal with it, there was no point getting into what she'd just learned about his marriage.

"I left a bail summary," he said, already glancing around the living room. "And Paul's gonna need— ah, there."

"I could've brought that," Anne told him, hoping her voice sounded steady. "You didn't have to drive all the way back here."

He looked startled as he reached for the folder on the coffee table. "Thanks. I didn't— Thanks."

Beth wouldn't have done that, she realized with a sudden jolt. Beth had resented his work.

Which made sense, considering how much of his attention it claimed. That aching sensation of *"I'm always going to come second!"* still resonated through her skin, and for a five-minutes-younger sister the awareness must have hurt even more. No wonder Beth had resented the legal clinic.

But, of course, a sister-in-law couldn't expect the same attention as a wife.

"If it comes up again," she offered, "just call me. I'll do whatever I can to help."

"I appreciate that," Rafe said, picking up the folder and meeting her gaze with an expression that, in anyone else, she might have described as...well, almost shy. "Anyway, back to work."

All right, that was good. That would give her another few hours to decide how much to say.

"You okay?" he asked, startling her again, and she fumbled for an answer.

Should she tell him about Beth's ring?

There was no way he could have noticed it missing, because after the fiery train wreck there'd been nothing but closed-casket funerals. But considering how devastated he'd been at the thought of Beth leaving him, what possible good could it do to mention that she'd discarded her wedding ring?

None, Anne decided. Yes, he had failed the woman who loved him…but he was suffering for that already.

Why make it worse?

"Fine," she answered hastily. "Everything's fine."

"You look like it's been a hard day."

He was right, and somehow his perception made it easier to keep quiet about his wife's frustration. No matter how guarded he might be with his feelings, no matter how frustrating it might be if you wanted his baby to bring you closer together, this man had been through enough.

He didn't need any more grief.

And surely her sister would say the same thing, because Beth wanted the best for the people she loved.

"It hasn't been that hard a day," she said, remembering with a pang his anguished confession that Beth had wanted more than he could give. She had, yes, but how much *could* one man give? "Rafe, don't worry about me. Just worry about the clinic kids."

"Already on it," he said, and gave her an appreciative smile as he turned toward the door. "Okay, then, I'll see you later."

Probably much later, but she'd leave his dinner ready for whenever he finally made it home. Because there wasn't much else she could do for this man.

And it wasn't like he wanted anyone taking care of him, anyway.

But she wanted to, Anne knew as she watched him head outside on his way back to Legalismo.

At least for four more weeks, she wanted to care for him the way he deserved.

Not like a wife, no. Not in his bed, and with any luck she'd be too tired for those dreams tonight.

But *someone* needed to care for Rafe Montoya.

And for the next four weeks, that someone would be her.

She was so easy to be with, Rafe reflected as he returned to the clinic with Paul's file. And again when he came home shortly before midnight, only to find a plate of lasagna in the refrigerator and a heating-instruction note in the handwriting that he always mistook for his wife's.

She was amazing.

Remarkably like Beth in her capacity for nurturing, and yet completely different in how readily she accepted the demands of Legalismo.

Which had grown a lot more intense tonight, with Cholo's unspoken request for assistance on the kind of case he'd dreamed of for years.

Put it aside, Rafe ordered himself.

Wait until tomorrow.

He punched the microwave numbers on her note, remembering how he'd enjoyed Beth's practice of leaving dinner for him during the first few months of their marriage...until he realized he was coming to depend on it, and convinced her to stop. Probably it was better, even now, not to let himself spend too much time enjoying the luxury of a home-cooked dinner at midnight.

Because even if his fantasy *were* a reality—

No, that would mean the kind of miracle he knew better than to expect.

Put that aside, too.

It was getting harder, though, he admitted as he watched the lighted seconds tick past, to keep dismissing the hope that somehow Beth had survived the train wreck. That somehow a whole team of medics and a longtime friend had mixed up the twins.

Not too likely.

But he'd phoned the trauma team this morning, anyway, just to see whether an identification error might have been possible.

Only to learn that the crew chief was out for a few days.

"I could let you talk to his deputy," the clerk offered, "but if you want somebody with the answers, you'd be better off waiting for Don."

So he was waiting.

Waiting for the chime of the microwave.

Waiting to get over this pointless longing for a chance to make things right with his wife.

Waiting for Don to explain that mistakes of that caliber didn't happen.

Any more than miracles did.

And he should know that by now. After Mom walked out, after Nita parked him with the neighbors, when Gramp collapsed, when Carlos was killed, when Rose took off after promising to love him forever…it was stupid, Rafe had learned through experience, to hope for miracles in a world like that.

But he was still hoping three days later when Don returned his call, and in spite of the crew chief's insistence that such a mistake was highly unlikely, he pressed hard enough to win the chief's promise of follow-up calls to everyone on the trauma team.

"Rafe, are you finished yet?" Heidi, who'd been poking her head in every few minutes, came into his office and shut the door behind her. "We might have a situation out there. This guy Cholo wants to see you, but he won't come in without his gun."

All right, a problem he could fix. Reality rather than fantasy. "I'm on it," he said, and went to deal with the gang leader who—please, God—might finally be ready to ask for help.

"Hey, this is important," Cholo announced as soon as Rafe came into the lobby. "I know you got your rules, but—"

"Out here," Rafe said, guiding him with an arm around his shoulders to the sidewalk outside the front door. "Okay, is your cousin ready for a lawyer?"

Cholo's cousin, Billy, had been arrested for murder the other night after a party, which had drawn probably half the street kids in South Tucson.

"I told you, they're trying to get *me*," the Lobos leader said. "But I don't want to talk about it out here. We need some privacy."

"Your call." He couldn't show how badly he wanted this case, how certain he felt that this might be his ticket into proving Legalismo could be trusted. "I'll be around most of the day."

Cholo stared at him, the intimidating stare Rafe had used himself whenever the situation required. "Billy didn't do it."

"Yeah, you mentioned that." They could do the whole intake here on the sidewalk and let the guy save face, but sooner or later there would have to be a showdown. He turned back toward the door, hoping he looked as casual as if this were just another potential client who might or might not return. "If you want us to work on it, let me know."

The gang leader waited until he was almost inside before muttering, "Tonight."

"I'll be here," Rafe agreed, keeping his posture relaxed. "Same rules, but there's more privacy."

What were the odds, he wondered as he went inside and saw Heidi's troubled gaze follow Cholo down the street, that the gang leader would be back tonight with the gun and a couple of knives?

Pretty good. But he could work around that. Stay on the sidewalk, start the intake, get the guy involved, then recommend going inside to phone a judge—and deal with the weapons again.

"You think he'll come back later?" the intern asked.

"I hope so." From what he'd heard, Billy was nothing more than a convenient scapegoat, and the chance to clear an innocent kid while establishing Legalismo as a credible force was too good to miss. "See if you can get me the police report, okay? I want this to work right from the start."

"You think he'll be back if he can't bring a gun in?"

"I hope so," he repeated, and realized as he returned to his desk that today was all about hope. If he could just fix things with the trauma team, same as he hoped to do with Cholo and Billy—

But hope was never enough.

He needed to take some action. Something beyond just wishing Beth had survived. Because if she had...

If she had, Rafe vowed as he gazed at her photo on his desk, things would be different this time. Given a second chance, he would fix things right away. Do whatever it took to keep Beth happy.

And if that meant starting a family with the clinic still on shaky ground, well, then, they'd start a family.

Somehow or other, he would make time for fatherhood.

Whatever it took.

But he was getting way ahead of himself, he realized as he jerked his gaze away from the picture. After all, there was absolutely no evidence of mistaken identity.

Nothing but his own desire...which had never been enough to work a miracle before.

"Rafe, Oscar wants you to call him."

Action. Right. Rafe reached for the phone, then stopped.

If he wanted evidence of a mistake, damn it, he needed to pursue this the way he'd pursue any other investigation. Find someone else who might know something. Forget the trauma team, he'd done everything he could on that front. He needed someone who might—

Jake Roth.

Where had the guy called from, New York? Boston? Boston, he remembered, and picked up the phone book. And within half an hour, he found himself talking to Jake Roth's wife.

"Of course I remember Anne's brother-in-law,"

she told him. "We spoke last month, remember, when Jake and I kept phoning the hospital? How is she?"

This was going to be tricky, Rafe realized, gazing again at the photo of Beth smiling at his Legalismo sign on the clinic's first day. There was no good way of asking whether Jake might've been blind, or stupid, or both.

"Still having some problems with her memory," he answered, setting aside his own memory of kissing Beth after she'd hung the sign on the front door. "And I thought it might help to know more about the train wreck."

"Well, I'm sure Jake would be happy to help," the woman offered. "He'll be back in a few hours, if you want me to have him call you?"

"Yeah, thanks." Rafe gave her the clinic number, knowing there was no point in upsetting Anne with a call about the biggest trauma of her life. "I just have a couple of questions."

More than a couple, but he had to start someplace. And with that out of the way, he could return his attention to Oscar.

Then to the girl who hadn't seen her boyfriend since he left in her car.

And the gardener who needed a paycheck his boss kept losing.

And the father worried about his ex-wife's arrest record.

It was a typical day, but he felt more energetic than he'd felt in a while. Even though he was probably setting himself up for a massive disappointment, he couldn't help enjoying the whisper of hope flickering under his skin.

The possibility of another chance.

Because if Beth was alive, things would be different this time. He would make up for all his past failures to make her feel loved.

Show her she mattered.

Even give her a baby. Cindy had repeatedly warned against strenuous exercise, but the question of pregnancy had never come up.

Regardless, though…this time, he'd get it right.

When the phone rang, he made himself draw a deep breath before grabbing it. He couldn't browbeat the witness, elicit the answers he wanted by sheer force of will. All he needed was the possibility of a mistake, and then…

Then he'd figure out what to do next.

"Sorry to hear Anne's still having problems," Jake told him. "Mindy said it might help her, hearing about that morning."

"Just a thought," Rafe said. "I know you were with her when it happened, but did you see her sister anywhere?"

"That was your wife, right? No, sorry…I didn't even know they were traveling together, until Mindy talked to you at the hospital."

Okay, but that didn't necessarily mean anything. And there was really no way to find out what he needed, Rafe decided, other than a direct question.

"What I'm wondering is, might Anne and Beth have gotten mixed up?"

"You mean, was I talking to Beth?" Jake sounded intrigued. "I never met her, but I'd swear that was Anne. I'd know her anywhere."

By appearance, maybe, but—aside from their hair

and wardrobe—her appearance was the same as Beth's. "Did she know who you were?"

"Well, I thought so. But I might've said my name when she first came in." Another pause. "Doesn't she know who she is?"

"Everyone's been telling her she's Anne." Which was only logical, since she'd been sporting Anne's haircut, carrying Anne's purse, wearing Anne's ring—

Why would Beth be wearing her sister's ring?

"Maybe you should ask her if she's really your wife," Jake suggested. "Seems like if she is, she'd want to know."

"Yeah, maybe so." Although, considering how she'd been listing the pros and cons of divorce, she might have deliberately suppressed any awareness of her marriage—

Even traded rings with Anne? Swapping her wedding band for something else?

Oh, God.

He was going to lose her again.

If she was even Beth in the first place...

"Thanks," Rafe said hoarsely, and managed to finish the call without letting his voice crack. What the hell was he doing, setting himself up for another loss?

No, it was a long shot to begin with.

It was a fantasy, nothing more.

He was getting in way over his head, feeling the same yearning for his wife's sister that he'd once felt for his wife, and trying to make it okay by pretending that Beth had survived.

Not only survived, but wanted to keep their marriage together.

Pretending didn't work, he knew.

Neither did bargaining with God.

But even so, he found himself clutching the medal in his pocket.

This time, I'll get it right.

Just give me another chance.

This time, she won't be lonely. I promise.

This time, I'll get it right.

This wasn't like her, Anne knew.

She wasn't the kind of person who woke up dreaming about a man. Who spent hours thinking of his smile. Who found herself basking in the awareness that, whether he realized it or not, he needed her.

She wasn't the kind of person who fell in love.

But she was perilously close to loving her sister's husband.

"It's just stress," she told Cindy, bracing her shoulders against the table in preparation for the countdown. "Of course my heart rate's too fast, because I'm worried about all the work backing up in Chicago. So I'm distracting myself by planning what to cook for dinner."

"Cooking can be relaxing," the therapist offered. "There's nothing wrong with that."

No, of course not. But Beth was the one who took care of home and family.

Not Anne.

Not the career woman who'd taken a doll-making business and turned it into a sizeable corporation.

Not the woman with a perfectly good job and a perfectly good life in Chicago, regardless of how faint they might be in her memory right now. Once she got back to her real life, all these feelings for Rafe would vanish like bubbles.

All she needed was her job back.

"I've just never been much of a homemaker," she explained, although it felt strange saying those words. "But, I don't know, lately it's like I care about different things than I used to."

"That happens, remember? A lot of times, people who've gone through some kind of trauma start making changes in their life."

Changes, yes. But not the kind of change it would take to fall in love with Beth's husband.

With some other man, maybe...

"So," Cindy continued, "whatever matters to you now, you might as well plan on making it part of your life. Go back to Chicago and plant a garden. Get a puppy. Something like that."

If it would make her stop dreaming about Rafe, she'd be looking through the singles-wanted ads right now. But the very idea made her cringe. Her sister could do that with no problem, but—

No, wait. Beth wasn't the type to look through singles ads, either.

"Nineteen, twenty," the therapist concluded, and she let her muscles relax. "Now the other side."

She wasn't going shopping for a man, no matter what. Not when she had her job to get back to.

Not when she had Rafe to look after.

"You really *are* tense," Cindy observed, adjusting the weight levers. "Have you been getting enough sleep?"

"I stayed up kind of late last night." She'd woken at one-thirty and again at four, flushed with heat and afraid to remember what she'd been dreaming. Even though some of the dreams were respectable enough, like the one about buying Rafe's shirts, she didn't need any reminders of what had danced through her mind last night. "Maybe I need some more exercise."

"Activity," Cindy corrected her. "I don't want you pushing your muscles any more than you're already doing, but if you wanted to go for a walk or see a movie or something like that, it might be good."

She didn't really want to do any of those things alone. Of course, some of Beth's friends had invited her to lunch "anytime that's convenient," but taking over more of her sister's life was a bad idea. And while Rafe would probably insist on driving if she mentioned a movie, she didn't want him escorting her, either.

Maybe what she needed was to meet some other man…. "I'll think about it," she said.

"Listen, if you want to come to Jeff's poetry reading tonight, he'd be thrilled to see a friendly face."

Cindy's boyfriend had scheduled his first performance in a coffeehouse near the university, and she'd been describing his plans all week.

"Maybe I will." Rafe would likely be gone until midnight, anyway, and she ought to at least try some activity that would give her dreams a different direction. "If I can make it, I'll be there by eight."

She was there by seven-thirty, feeling a little nervous until she noticed that her new jeans and white lacy top matched the general style of dress. All right, then, at least she'd fit in with the crowd. And if she wound up acquiring some memories to push Rafe Montoya out of her mind, so much the better.

If not, at least she could enjoy the coffee of the day.

Which she did, along with an evening of poetry, guitar music and easy chat with a handful of people.

Including two men who asked for her phone number.

It shouldn't surprise her, but it did. Apparently she didn't strike anyone else as the kind of woman who spent every free minute pining over her brother-in-law. A woman who enjoyed the sensation of being needed far more than she would ever admit.

"I'll be leaving for Chicago in another few weeks," she told both men, but the one named Greg didn't seem to mind.

"We'll get together before you leave," he suggested, so she gave him the number and wondered what would happen if he phoned while Rafe was at home.

Probably nothing. Probably Rafe would hand her the phone with the same reflexive courtesy he showed to every caller.

But at least she would know she'd done her best to arrange a distraction from those increasingly detailed dreams.

"Call me," she ordered, and left before she could change her mind. The drive home would give her plenty of time to fix Greg's image in her memory, and maybe tomorrow she'd wake up without any of that embarrassing warmth inside her.

The drive home didn't take quite long enough, though, because she was still thinking of Rafe when she walked inside. And when she found him waiting for her at the front door, with every light in the house glowing a welcome, she felt a curious sense of comfort.

Until he rested his hands on her shoulders, met her gaze with a look that bordered on panic and demanded, ''Where the hell have you been?''

Chapter Six

"At a coffeehouse," she blurted, and Rafe felt his muscles tighten. Fine, she'd left a note about some poetry reading, but that didn't erase the shock of coming home and finding her gone.

"Are you all right?" he asked, and she took a step back, looking startled.

"I'm fine! What's the matter, didn't you get my note?"

"Yeah, two hours ago. But—" He broke off. This wasn't any of his business, and of course she had every right to go wherever she wanted, but he'd be damned if he was going to lose her.

Which didn't make sense. She had her life in Chicago, and of course he was going to lose her.

So what the hell was he *thinking,* anyway?

Just…

"I was worried about you," he muttered.

Her expression softened, and she gave him that familiar smile as she moved past him into the living room. "That's nice of you. But you've got enough to worry about with the clinic kids."

She was right about that, but it didn't seem to make any difference. "I don't know," Rafe admitted, "when I got home and you weren't here, it kind of threw me. I mean, I know you can take care of yourself, but—"

He stopped himself again.

Saying *he* wanted to take care of her might be way out of line.

"But you weren't expecting the house to be empty," she finished for him, setting down her bright red purse on the coffee table and turning to face him again. "I should've phoned you at Legalismo."

Damn right.

"No," he managed to say, trying not to notice the way she moved, the flicker of lace against her skin. "You don't have to report to me. I just— No. Never mind."

She drew a long breath, then sat down on the sofa, exactly the way Beth would have. "Want to hear about the poetry reading?"

He ought to let her get to bed, but he couldn't turn down an offer of conversation. Not when she seemed as wide-awake as he felt.

"Sure," Rafe said, and settled on the other end of the sofa. Not close enough for any accidental touch, because the way she looked tonight, he didn't quite trust himself right now. "Tell me about it."

"Well..." She seemed more sparkly, more glow-

ing than he'd seen her over the past few weeks.
"Cindy's boyfriend was making his first appearance
ever. I didn't think he was that good, but I don't know
much about poetry."

Neither did he. Neither had Beth, and they had
laughed about that.

"And there was a guitar player who was really
good. It was at this coffeehouse, down by the university."

He could imagine her there, wearing that lacy
blouse, drawing every eye in the place.

"Yeah," Rafe said slowly. Of course she had every
right to wear whatever she wanted, to go wherever
she wanted, but... "Was there much of a crowd?"

"Oh, twenty or thirty people." Then she dropped
her gaze. "I didn't talk to all of them."

Just a few, he thought with a twist in his gut. And
every last one of them had wanted her.

"But this one guy might call," she continued, and
he could see a faint flush of color on her neck. "I
don't know, maybe not."

"The way you look tonight?" His voice sounded
darker than he'd intended, but somehow he couldn't
seem to manage a casual tone. "He'll call."

"Well..." She shrugged, looking down at her
hands in her lap. "That was the idea, I guess."

None of his business, he knew that, but the idea of
some other guy calling her made his skin feel tight.

"If you don't mind my asking," Rafe muttered,
"what, exactly, were you trying to do?"

She let out a sharp sigh, as if the answer should be
obvious. "I was trying to get my mind off *you!*"

Oh.

Before he could react, she ducked her head. "No, forget I said that." Then, while he was still reeling under the impact of such a revelation, she returned her gaze to his. "I'm sorry," she said, pressing her hands against her thighs as if struggling for calm. "This is my problem, not yours."

No, it wasn't.

Not hers alone, anyway.

And even though he shouldn't take pleasure in knowing they shared the same problem, it was a relief to know she felt the same way.

"Same here," Rafe admitted. "It's not just you."

For a moment he saw a look of hope in her eyes, then she shook her head. "No, this isn't the same thing. You're not having these dreams."

He never remembered his dreams, although Beth had occasionally woken him from what she said sounded like a nightmare. "What dreams?"

"I just—" She hesitated. Looked at her hands again, as if searching for an acceptable answer. Then drew a quick breath, and met his gaze with an expression of relief. "Okay, here's one. The other night, I dreamed I was Beth."

Oh, God.

"I mean," she faltered, "sort of. I was with you at the clinic opening, putting the sign on the door."

Either she'd seen that picture on his desk, or he was sitting across from his wife.

A wife who'd wanted to leave him...but he couldn't think about that now. Just think about her hanging the Legalismo sign on the door.

"Beth did that," he said softly, watching her eyes for a glimmer of recognition.

But nothing happened. Instead she countered, "Beth, not me. Don't you see? I need to get my own life!"

All right, maybe now was the time to ask. Not quite as abrupt a question as "Could you be Beth?" but something that would jiggle her memory.

"Maybe," he offered slowly, "there's a reason you're dreaming like Beth."

She closed her eyes for a moment, and he saw a look of dismay on her face.

"It's like I'm trying to take over her life," she said in a small voice, "and I've got to figure out some way to stop. I thought if I quit wearing her clothes, quit using her shampoo, that'd do the trick."

Obviously it hadn't, and he wished he could spare her the pain he heard in her voice. No matter who this woman was, she didn't deserve this kind of confusion, this kind of hurt.

"Look," Rafe began, trying to keep any sign of tension from his voice, "this is gonna sound strange, okay? But maybe—"

"I know," she interrupted before he could finish the question, "maybe part of her spirit is alive in me. I've thought about that."

God, she'd been dealing with some pretty deep stuff. And she'd been doing it without any help from him.

Beth or Anne, either way, he needed to make things easier on her.

"I mean," she continued, "we share the same genes, and all that. It makes sense. But I think it's more just that I need to make some changes in my life."

All right, whatever she needed. Whatever she wanted. But he couldn't help hoping those changes would involve discovering that she was really his wife.

And that this time, he could make everything right.

"What kind of changes?" he managed to ask.

"Well..." She blushed again, and he found himself wishing he could touch her. Just take her hand. But if this wasn't Beth, he'd be lighting a fire that had no business burning.

"Changes like?" he prompted, and she drew a shaky breath.

"Like going out tonight. I need to stop wanting—" She faltered, caught herself before saying "you," but he could hear the admission as clearly as if she'd spoken it instead of a last-minute substitute. "Wanting Beth's life."

The knowledge sizzled through his veins like the most potent drug he'd ever tried. She wanted him as much as he wanted her, and the best he could do for both of them was to quit drawing this out.

Just confirm it, one way or another.

Right now.

"Let me ask you something, okay?" If there were a way of checking without arousing her suspicions, he might have opted for a less direct approach, but all he could do was ask. "Do you have a scar on your thigh?"

She glanced at her jeans, as if wondering how he might know what lay beneath the denim, but he couldn't see any confirmation in her puzzled expression. "Why?"

If this was Beth, she might appreciate how the story

unfolded. And if not, he would never let himself remember it again.

Which made the right beginning even more important.

"Tell you what," Rafe said. With the hope of recovery so close, he found himself more nervous than he'd been since proposing marriage almost three years ago. "Let's get something to drink, and I'll tell you about what happened on Christmas."

If she were smart, she'd make some excuse and get away right now. Because for some reason, maybe just the stimulation of the coffee this evening, she was having a hard time keeping her hands to herself.

And an even harder time keeping her eyes off Rafe.

But she couldn't resist the opportunity for another hour together, and his suggestion of getting a drink implied that whatever Christmas story he wanted to tell was a long one.

"Okay, sure," she said, and followed him to the kitchen. "No more coffee for me, though."

"Water with lemon, right?"

He'd been more observant than she realized, if he'd noticed what she drank after her sessions with Cindy. "I'll get it," she told him, and cut a wedge of lemon while he filled two glasses with bottled water. "Now, tell me the story."

Rafe took his usual seat at right angles to her, and flexed his hands together as if preparing a statement before a jury. "All right," he said slowly. "Christmas morning, right? We're opening presents together, the first time."

He must be talking about himself and Beth, because his first time opening presents with family members wouldn't be such a distinct memory.

Nor such a pleasant one, because his family hadn't been all that stable.

"Right," she said, squeezing the lemon into her water and taking a sip. This promised to be a long story, and the way she was feeling right now, she could listen to him talk all night. Just talk, nothing more. Math theorems, baseball scores, it didn't matter as long as she could listen to his low, leisurely voice. "Opening presents."

"So one of the best was an instant camera, where you can take pictures and see 'em twenty seconds later." There was something almost hypnotic in his tone, something that made her want to drink in every word. "And we took that with us to Sabino Canyon."

"Hiking," she murmured. Beth must have told her about that, because she had a very clear memory of the desert canyon trail lined with saguaros and mesquite. "I know."

"All right, so we're wandering off the main road, just kind of looking at the scenery. Taking pictures, goofing around...you know how everything seems funny when you're having a good time."

Yes, she knew. She could almost hear their laughter, in fact, and his insistence that taking pictures of him was a waste of film.

"Anyway," he continued, still watching her with that steady, intriguing gaze, "after a while we've used up the camera, so we decide it's time for a picnic. Sandwiches, nothing fancy, just whatever was in the kitchen."

Leftovers, right. "Turkey and Swiss cheese."

Rafe nodded in acknowledgment, and a curious light flickered in his eyes. "I had a blanket in the car—you know, that old blue one? It was pretty beat-up."

Pretty beat-up, yes. The car *and* the blanket.

"So we spread it out in this clearing," he continued. "Mesquite bushes all over the place, but we didn't really care. It was off the trail a ways, and we had some privacy."

The image of privacy was the most vivid one yet, because she could see the blanket-size clearing, surrounded by a screen of those tiny-leafed bushes, with the clear desert sky overhead and the vast tranquility of nature in every direction. "No other hikers wandering by."

He nodded again, still with that same intensity in his gaze. "So we unpack our lunch, pretty slowly, because we're ready for a break. And we're enjoying it, knowing we've got all the time in the world...."

"Yes," she breathed. The way he told this story was so perfect, so real, she could actually feel herself right there with him. Enjoying the sunshine, enjoying the leisure.

Enjoying the anticipation.

"And we're both getting more excited, you know? Nobody out here, we're in the middle of nature, and if we want to stay here all day we can do that. So that's great, we're ready, we've got all the time we want...but we're starting to get impatient, right? Because we want to keep on kissing each other, touching each other, except our clothes are getting in the way."

His Christmas-gift shirt. Her new black jeans. Getting in the way, yes, and the desert boots making it even worse.

"But now, finally, we've gotten rid of everything, and there's nothing but us and the blanket and we're all over each other, we don't even notice the sun or the sky or the bushes—"

No, because all that mattered was celebration, the heat between them, the glorious arch and thrust and fulfillment and joy.

"We don't notice anything except each other," Rafe said hoarsely, "and that's all we care about. That's all I care about. Except I should've noticed we're too close to the bushes, because there's this one sharp branch and that's my fault, it winds up gouging—"

"That didn't matter!"

He stopped. Caught his breath.

"It didn't," she repeated. "I didn't even notice it, remember?"

A pulsing silence.

"But," he said, "it left a scar."

Yes, but that was her picnic souvenir. It—

It was—

It's mine.

My scar.

"*My* picnic souvenir." Beth's, not Anne's. "Rafe, this is—" She felt a rush of dizziness, and he was immediately at her side, his arm around her shoulders, holding her steady as the realization flooded through her in a sudden surge of elation. "Rafe, it's me!"

"Beth." His whisper was a confirmation, an exultation, a prayer of wonder. "You're back. You're here."

Here with him, here at the kitchen table they'd picked out together, here in a jumble of disbelief and memories and the bewildering certainty that she belonged with this man. It didn't make sense, she was supposed to be Anne, but in spite of that, whoever she was belonged here.

Right here.

"I *belong* here," she told him, and he gathered her into a rushing embrace. "I don't know what happened, but—"

"But you're alive," he murmured, running his hands through her hair as if he couldn't get enough of her against his skin. "God. Oh, God. Thank you. Beth."

It felt strange, hearing her name on his lips. Familiar and right, but strange. "You thought I was Anne. *I* thought I was Anne." How could they have thought that? "Anne's in Chicago."

She felt his sudden tension before he made a deliberate effort to relax the tightness of his hold on her, but even as he caught his breath she realized the truth.

"No, wait. She died instead of me."

Rafe let out a shaky breath. "I'm sorry. You shouldn't have to go through losing your sister twice."

All this time, she'd been grieving for the wrong person. But the feeling hadn't changed, Beth realized with another twinge of the aching loneliness that had haunted her all along. Regardless of the name, the sister she'd lost was her birthmate…and the name didn't make any difference.

Everything else, though, was incredibly different.

Rafe was her husband, and this was her home.

She belonged here. With the familiar clothes, with the dishes she'd chosen, with the vanilla shampoo that she'd thought belonged to her sister. With the man she'd thought belonged to her sister.

The man she couldn't stop dreaming about.

"Rafe," she said, drawing back so she could look at him face-to-face—oh, his face! "I missed you so much."

His eyes, usually so dark, were filled with a new shimmer of light. "I missed you, too. I kept hoping it was you, only— My God, Beth, I didn't think miracles happened."

The awe on his face warmed her heart. He loved her, it was obvious, and somehow she'd lost track of that during the past few weeks while trying to keep her distance from Rafe Montoya.

But she didn't have to keep her distance any longer. With a burst of happiness overshadowing the persistent ache of loss, she threw herself back into his arms and gloried in the familiar sensation.

This, this was what she'd been dreaming of.

Or at least part of it. And even if she would never see her sister again, she would still have this man. Because, Beth thought with a flash of relief, they belonged together.

Now.

Here.

"I think," she said breathlessly, "we need to make sure my picnic souvenir is still there."

Although his eyes still held a look of reverence, his flashing smile was purely male. "Good idea."

Oh, and they could share their own bed! Not the guest bed where she'd slept alone all this time, but the bed where she belonged. If they could even make it that far down the hall, and right now she wasn't too sure.

But Rafe seemed sure enough for both of them, because with one swift move he lifted her into his arms and started down the hall.

Then hesitated.

"Just one thing," he muttered. "I can't— As soon as we know it's safe, then we're fine."

What? She wriggled in his embrace, trying to get a better look at his expression. What was he talking about?

"A baby," he said, meeting her gaze with a look of promise. "Beth, we'll start a family the minute we hear it's okay. I should've asked Cindy, is it safe for you to get pregnant—"

"You mean it?" If ever there was a night of miracles, this was it. With a family, she would never be lonely again. "Rafe, you're ready for a baby?"

"As soon as we know it's safe," he repeated, holding her closer against him and continuing toward their room. "First thing tomorrow, if we can get Dr. Sibley on the phone. But for tonight, just let me hold you."

But that wasn't enough! That wasn't nearly enough, not with all the miracles shimmering in the air around them. "No, come on," she protested as he carried her through the bedroom door. "It's safe right now, my pills are—"

Oh.

No.

For the past few weeks, she hadn't even thought about birth control. But Rafe was always preaching safe sex to the street kids. "Don't you have any condoms?"

"I wish I did," he said, gently setting her down on the bed from her dreams. "I used to keep 'em in my car, but—"

"*My* car!" She sat up, stammering with excitement. "In the glove compartment. The other day, I saw it. One of those kits you give out."

"Yeah?" There was a new huskiness in his voice, a rough awareness that filled her with anticipation. "I'll be right back. And, Beth…" He rested his hands on her shoulders for a moment, letting the pulsing warmth between them rise even higher, then drew back with a strangled oath, as if the heat were growing too strong to resist. "Don't move."

She had moved, Rafe saw when he got back. He'd been gone for only a minute, but she had already fluffed up her hair and stripped off her jeans. Stripped off everything, in fact, except that lacy white top.

Which was enough to leave him breathless, right there.

But that wasn't all. She'd turned off the bedroom lamp, as well, and started lighting the chunky white candles on the dresser. Filling the air with a faint, shimmering light that left his senses tingling.

And when she looked up from the half-lit candles and saw him at the doorway, he felt as if there was a thread of pure energy vibrating between them, heating the entire room with its sheer intensity.

For a moment they both stood still, staring at one another, and then he saw her blush.

Rafe shoved the kit in his pocket, never taking his

eyes off her. This woman was incredible, the way she faced him with such eager warmth and yet with such shy hesitation. Even so, her intention was vividly clear.

And wonderfully welcome.

"You moved," he said.

Her color deepened, and she set down the unlit candle with slightly shaky hands. "I wanted to make things…special."

She had.

She was.

"You're already special," he said softly, crossing the room and letting himself touch the pale skin along the back of her neck the way he'd dreamed of the past few days. It felt like an eternity that he'd been keeping his distance, avoiding any touch at all, and now that he knew it was safe he wanted to take it slowly. Make it last.

Make it good.

At first she leaned closer to him with a shiver of pleasure, but then she pulled back and picked up the matches again, as if she had a mission to complete. "I figured we've had these candles for ages," she said, and he could hear a tremor in her voice. "We might as well use them."

She was nervous, he realized with a mixture of amazement and tenderness. It was strange to see Beth at a loss for composure, but the unexpected sweetness of it warmed his heart.

"No rush," he said gently, moving back a step and watching her light the next candle. "We've got all the time in the world."

She recognized the phrase, he could tell, because

NO POSTAGE
NECESSARY
IF MAILED
IN THE
UNITED STATES

BUSINESS REPLY MAIL
FIRST-CLASS MAIL   PERMIT NO. 717-003   BUFFALO, NY

POSTAGE WILL BE PAID BY ADDRESSEE

SILHOUETTE READER SERVICE
3010 WALDEN AVE
PO BOX 1867
BUFFALO NY 14240-9952

If offer card is missing write to: The Silhouette Reader Service, 3010 Walden Ave., P.O. Box 1867, Buffalo, NY 14240-1867

Play the Lucky Hearts Game

and get...

2 FREE BOOKS
and a **FREE MYSTERY GIFT**...

YOURS to KEEP!

yes! I have scratched off the silver card.
Please send me my **2 FREE BOOKS** and
FREE mystery GIFT. I understand that I am
under no obligation to purchase any books as
explained on the back of this card.

Scratch Here!
then look below to see
what your cards get you...
2 Free Books & a Free
Mystery Gift!

335 SDL D34T   **235 SDL D35A**

FIRST NAME	LAST NAME

ADDRESS

APT.#   CITY

STATE/PROV.   ZIP/POSTAL CODE   (S-SE-10/04)

Twenty-one gets you
2 FREE BOOKS
and a **FREE MYSTERY GIFT!**

Twenty gets you
2 FREE BOOKS!

Nineteen gets you
1 FREE BOOK!

TRY AGAIN!

she gave him a sudden smile, still fumbling with the pack of matches. "I guess we do at that."

"Can I give you a hand?" He took the matches from her and lit the last three candles, marveling at her gift for making their familiar bedroom into someplace entirely new. For making her*self* into someone new, with that lacy garment he'd never seen before sending a clear, definite invitation. "You're amazing, you know that?"

"Well," she murmured without quite meeting his gaze, "this is kind of like our first time. And the other first time, remember, you were worried about hurting me? So this time, I want it to be…you know. Better."

He felt a swell of awe, a surge of humility mingled with pride—that this woman could care so much! "Ah, Beth," he breathed, placing his hands on her shoulders for one quick kiss.

Just one, he reminded himself as she raised her face to his.

Just one short kiss. But already it seemed as if it would never stop. He could feel her melting into the lines of his body, fitting against him so perfectly that it seemed she had always been a part of him, and with a sweet rush of longing he slid his hands down her back to pull her hips against his.

Beth, yes!

He teased her lips with his tongue, and she responded with a shiver of pleasure. Gently, he circled her mouth, sharing the heady enjoyment of exploring one another with promising leisure, knowing they had all the time in the world.

With his eyes closed, his other senses seemed all the clearer, and he feasted on the sensation of her so close, so yielding in his arms that it seemed she had always belonged there. She did, Rafe knew, and he belonged with her, floating in this world of warmth and softness and joy, such joy! Such richness, such sweetness, such sheer and utter rightness that he knew his life had been waiting, only waiting for this.

For now.

For her.

"Beth," he whispered again, loving the sound of her name on his lips. "This is already the best we've ever been."

She murmured a sound of agreement, pressing her hips closer to his and setting off another surge of heat. He could feel it rising between them, enveloping them both in a growing swirl of warmth that arched over his skin, increased the pulse of his heart and made him clutch her even more tightly against him.

This, he realized with a sudden explosion of yearning, was everything he wanted. This was sustenance, this was light. This was raw and ancient fire, and it leaped so high, so fast that he wondered with what little sense remained whether they could even make it as far as the bed. He wanted her there, yes, but five feet away was too far when he wanted her now, here, now!

"Oh, yes," Beth murmured against his chest, and the half-heard sound sent him plummeting over the edge of reason, into a whirlwind of hunger and promise and force. All he needed, all he wanted was her. All of her, right here.

Right now.

He fumbled with the lace at her shoulders and felt her writhe in response, trying to make it easier for him to slide the garment off her and down to the floor, out of the way—there, yes—and all the while she was doing the same for him, tugging at the clothes between them as if tearing down walls that had stood for too long. Far too long, Rafe thought dizzily, torn between helping her and helping himself tear away every last scrap of resistance.

There were too many clothes to get rid of smoothly, but right now neither one of them cared about grace. All that mattered was sensation, skin soft and rough, breath hard and ragged, hands hot and eager for the next touch, the next embrace, the next surge of desire. Rafe lowered her to the floor before the wave could crest over them, then grabbed a handful of discarded clothing to thrust under her hips.

"Now," he gasped as she rose to meet his touch— yes, she wanted it as much as he did, she felt the same crackling tension—but it was happening so fast, so fast! He should slow down, he should draw this out a little longer, but he couldn't keep his hands from her, he couldn't stop now.

Not with her reaching for him, so warm and so welcoming that he knew he would never want any other home.

Not with her matching his every move, every shift, every touch with one of her own.

Not with her so much softer, so much hotter, so much sweeter than he had let himself remember.

He couldn't stop now, Beth thought wildly. Not when his ardent touch was making her burn in places she'd never known existed. Not when his tongue, his hands, his entire body seemed to know exactly where she needed his fierce invasion. Another time she could wait, maybe, savoring the anticipation, but right now all she wanted was Rafe and the hot, hungry passion of him filling her to the very depths.

Now.

Yes.

Oh, now!

And finally, finally he was there, exactly where she wanted, moving with the swift and exhilarating certainty of welcome, straight into her very soul.

"Yes," she gasped, and felt him shiver in response. "Oh, Rafe, yes."

He echoed that plea with his own gasp, shuddering as the first impact swept over them both. But there was more to come, she knew with a frantic burst of need, because he still wasn't moving quite as hard or as fast or as deep as she wanted, until—

Oh. There. Yes.

"Yes," she cried again, and this time he was with her completely, filling every empty fragment of her with his own savage energy, his own demanding heat. Filling her perfectly, incredibly, beyond any boundaries of spirit or flesh or blood, filling her beyond measure of distance or ocean or sky. "Oh, yes, oh, Rafe, yes, oh!"

She felt him cry out at the same moment she did, felt him shatter inside her, and reached blindly for him so they could fall back to earth together.

A leisurely fall.

A long, swirling tumble through layers of cloud and cushions of air, drifting gradually closer back to the light and the scent of the candles and the clothes tangled beneath her. Back to their bedroom floor— what were they doing on the floor?—with the flickering light on the ceiling above them, casting random shadows on his skin as he lay panting beside her, still holding her as if he couldn't believe such richness would last.

"Don't let go," she whispered, and he drew her closer to him, cushioning her head in the curve of his shoulder and nestling her against the hard, sustaining warmth of his body.

"Beth." His voice was hoarse, thick with emotion, and she knew she'd glimpsed the side of Rafe Montoya that he rarely let escape. The softer, more vulnerable side. "My Beth…"

She belonged with him, she knew. Exactly like this.

And he belonged with her. Exactly like—

Well, maybe not exactly like this. Not on the floor all night, not when they had a perfectly good bed only a few steps away.

But moving to the bed would involve getting up, and neither of them was in any shape to get up right now.

So instead, she snuggled closer into his embrace and gently kissed the only part of him she could reach, the warm and salty skin of his chest where she could feel the pulse of his heartbeat.

"Good dreams," she whispered, and let them come.

Chapter Seven

"Come on," Rafe urged, coaxing her out of a sated sleep with the aroma of something like coffee. "If you don't sit up pretty soon, I'm gonna be right back in bed with you—and we used up the condoms last night."

They had, she remembered through a haze of satisfaction, trying to make sense of his words. Sitting up sounded like too much work, but maybe if she concentrated on the sound of his voice…

No, actually, his voice made her want to sink right back into bed with him on top of her.

So she'd better think about the coffee instead.

"Okay," she murmured, letting him help with a cushion of pillows against the headboard, then getting her first clear look at Rafe this morning.

He looked wonderful.

Even with a day's growth of whiskers roughening the line of his jaw, even with his hair still disheveled, the man was a pleasure to watch. He wore nothing but the jeans he'd worn last night, but as he turned to retrieve the coffee from the bedside table, she could see the dark swirl of hair inviting her touch, the taut muscles of his back and shoulders, and the faded gang tattoo on his left arm.

A tattoo he wanted to get rid of, she knew, once he could afford the procedure. But that kind of money would take a while to save, and she didn't mind the glimpse of his earlier life.

Or anything else.

"You look so good," she blurted, and Rafe shot her a startled glance.

"I should've let you sleep later," he teased, handing her the first mug of coffee and taking the other for himself. "You can't trust your eyes, first thing in the morning."

Maybe not, but she trusted her heart. She scooted sideways, making room for him next to her against the pillows, and he settled beside her with a sigh of contentment.

"Our first morning together," she told him. "Sort of."

"First enough." He took a sip of his coffee, then set it on the table again and ran his fingers along the side of her face. "I like your hair this way. Easier to play with."

That's right, he hadn't seen her new haircut in daylight yet. At least not while knowing it belonged to her.

"I got this whole makeover," she explained,

"while Anne and I were in California." Although, actually, that had been a bad idea. "Only I wish I hadn't, because otherwise you would've known right away it was me."

"I wanted it to be you," Rafe said soberly. "I kept telling myself to quit hoping, get over it, but I couldn't quite believe you were gone."

She felt a tremor of compassion—he'd lost so many people already!—and reached with her free hand to draw him closer to her. "Rafe, I'm so sorry. I wish you hadn't had to go through all that."

"Hey." He pulled back long enough to take her coffee mug and set it alongside his own, then covered both her hands with his. "I've got nothing to gripe about, for the rest of my life. You know? God hands you a miracle like that, you don't start whining about anything else."

Well, maybe not. She hadn't thought of it that way.

"I mean," he said, "that'd be like ignoring the best gift I'll ever get. If I go around griping 'why didn't they check the ID' and 'who got their rings mixed up,' it's like— I'm not doing that."

"Their rings mixed up…"

Oh, no.

She glanced at the *claddagh* ring she'd worn for the past several weeks, realizing with a pang that Rafe still didn't know about the decision to leave her own ring at home.

And his willingness to dismiss any blame or resentment, in exchange for the miracle of her return, was so humbling that she hated to bring up such a topic.

But she wanted her wedding ring back.

Now.

Because now that she had her husband again, it was time to retrieve the symbol of their marriage.

"Wait a minute," Beth said, and scooted off his side of the bed. She went to the dresser, switching Anne's ring onto her right hand, then took her wedding band from the jewelry box and brought it back to Rafe. "Put this on me."

He stared at it, then at her. "This looks like—"

"It is." She wished there were some way to avoid telling the story, which no longer mattered now that he wanted to share the bond of a baby, but a swift stab was better than a lingering lie between them. "I left it here when Anne and I went on vacation, all right? You saw that pro-and-con list about splitting up—" and how she regretted that now "—but, Rafe, I don't mean that anymore. None of it. I want to stay with you."

He swallowed, regarding her silently for a moment. Then, without speaking, he held out his arms.

Oh, yes.

With a surge of relief, she hurried back to him and threw herself into his embrace.

"I want you to stay with me," he murmured, holding her so close that she could feel the warmth of his skin against hers as he slid the ring onto her finger. "I never meant for you to be lonely, like on your list, but from now on it'll be different."

Different, yes. The shared warmth was already making her want him again, but this was too important a conversation to let either of them get distracted.

"I promise," Rafe told her, holding her gaze with

his, "it'll be better this time. You'll see. I'm going to fix things."

"You already have." Forcing herself off the bed, she snatched his discarded shirt from the floor and directed her thoughts to what mattered most. "Just knowing you want a baby," she explained, sliding the shirt over her head and returning to her place beside him, "it's like you're putting our family first." And today she'd find out whether pregnancy counted as strenuous exercise, or whether they needed to wait another few months—but either way, she was finished with the pills.

He must have been reading her mind, Beth realized, because his response came without hesitation. "I want you to have whatever you want," he said simply, then confirmed it with a kiss. "I mean it."

She believed him, but he couldn't give her everything she wanted. "I just wish," she said with a catch in her throat as she gazed at her sister's ring, "Anne was still alive."

"So do I."

For a moment she felt her heart lurch, before realizing that he couldn't have meant that the way it sounded. It wasn't like he wished the other twin would come walking in right now. He only meant he wished that she had her sister back.

But the way he'd looked at her last night, while thinking she was Anne...

No, there was no point in remembering that.

"I need to say goodbye again," she told him, forcing the uneasiness aside and reaching for her coffee cup. "The whole time I was missing my sister, it's like I didn't know who I was missing." But now the memories of Anne were so clear, so vivid, that it was like losing her other half all over again. "Take her flowers for real this time."

"Sure," Rafe agreed. "We can go anytime you want." Then he winced, as if realizing an omission. "Except this afternoon, I've got some things to catch up on. Maybe I can get one of the interns—"

"No, that's okay," Beth interrupted. She couldn't expect him to give up a day of appointments he'd made before learning she was alive, but his look of guilt was proof that he meant for things to be different from now on. "I can go on my own. I think after the first few times, it won't hurt so much."

He regarded her soberly for a moment, then nodded, and she could see a shadow of darkness in his eyes. "It gets better."

"You know that from experience, don't you," she acknowledged. He had lost far more people than she had. His entire family, one by one, then the friend he'd counted as a brother and the girl to whom he'd given his heart. "Not just your parents, but everybody who—"

"Yeah, well," he said hastily, cutting her off before she could finish, "I've learned a lot. Made me stronger."

Although his tone was deliberately casual, she knew there was truth in the statement. "First time we met, that's what I noticed about you." He had stood out from everyone at the shelter, volunteers and clients alike, with his curious mixture of defiance and gallantry. "You've always been strong."

Rafe shrugged, dismissing the observation, and stood up. "That's what it takes to survive."

In the barrios where he'd grown up with rival gangs around every corner, probably so. But his tight posture implied that the danger was still nearby.

"Not anymore, though," she reminded him. "Not the way you live now."

He set to work gathering up last night's discarded clothes from the floor, and Beth slid out of bed to help. She'd have to move her things out of the guest room later, but for now all that mattered was keeping him company. Trying not to think about Anne just yet. Picking up her lacy blouse and looking in the closet for a hanger.

"But as a kid…" she continued, trying to keep her thoughts where they belonged. Rafe was what mattered. "You were Mr. Tough Guy even then, weren't you?"

He sounded more relaxed with a job at hand, dropping his and her underwear into the laundry hamper. "Same as Oscar is now," he agreed, then gave her a rueful smile. "Except Oscar still needs the gun."

"And you don't."

For a moment he didn't answer, but when she turned from the closet she saw him retrieving their coffee from the bedside table.

"It took me a while," he answered, "to figure that out." Then, along with her cup, he offered an explanation. "You need a knife, that's a sign of weakness. Taking care of people…that's strength."

"You," Beth told him, "are the strongest person I've ever known." Balancing her cup in one hand, she reached with the other to steady herself against his shoulder, and raised her face to his for a kiss. "I told my friends that first day at the homeless shelter, you were like a knight in shining armor. Saving the world.''

Rafe smiled at that, took a sip of his coffee, then shook his head. ''Right now I've got to save the world from cold coffee.''

He was right, she realized, and it was probably time to start taking the day seriously. Still, it would be lovely if they could start every morning with this kind of intimate conversation.

But one look at the clock showed they were already well past their usual departure time.

''I've got a session with Cindy,'' she admitted, setting her cup on the dresser and turning her attention to the issue of how fast they could both get showered and changed. And only then, with the realization that she no longer needed to confine herself to the guest bathroom, did it dawn on her that Cindy wouldn't know her patient had changed identities. ''She doesn't know who I am!''

''You're still you.''

Well, yes. ''But there's going to be a lot of stuff to straighten out.'' Her sister's apartment, the company, the headstone at the cemetery…the scope of the job seemed suddenly overwhelming.

And Rafe must have recognized that, because he swiftly gathered her into his arms and held her close. ''Beth,'' he said, ''it's okay. You don't have to worry about it.''

He sounded so calm, so comforting that she could almost feel her jangled nerves smoothing themselves out. She looked up at him, wondering how he could make such a sweeping promise, and saw him gazing at her with the same confidence she'd fallen in love with the first time they met.

"Remember," he murmured, "you've got a knight in shining armor."

A knight wouldn't let anything stand in his way.

Not a mountain of paperwork. Not floods of disbelief, hordes of bewildered clerks, nor dragons demanding proof that Anne Farrell was actually Beth Montoya.

His job was to protect her, as well as the Legalismo kids—yesterday's clash between the Lobos and Raptors meant heightened danger for them all—and her acceptance of that mission still warmed him.

Even though she seemed more concerned for his welfare now than when they thought she was Anne. "You're doing too much," Beth protested when he came home late for the second night in a row and found her already in bed. "Rafe, I know it's important work, but don't push yourself so hard."

"I'm okay," he assured her. With everything else she had to take care of, contacting all the friends who'd mourned her, the last thing Beth needed was to worry about him. "You've got enough on your plate, telling everyone you're alive again."

She dismissed that with a smile, which reassured him everything was still okay, that his late nights were no longer the problem they'd been three months ago. "It's kind of fun, though," she said as he deposited his keys on the dresser, "everybody saying how much they missed me. I'm having lunch with my old roommate on Friday, and Henry thinks I should take over Anne's job."

He felt a tremor of uneasiness. Maybe it was a senseless habit, especially since she'd apologized for that pro-and-con list, but for some reason he still dreaded the possibility of Beth walking out on him. "In Chicago?"

"No, I could keep working from here," she answered, sounding a little drowsy in spite of the bedside lamp which indicated she'd been up reading. "And I like the idea of doing something for her, because Anne's the one who made the company what it is."

"You should," he agreed through a rush of relief. Over the past few days he'd seen the shattering intensity of her grief whenever she recalled another memory of her sister, and it still seemed unfair that she should have to mourn twice. "Anything that'll make you feel better."

"I don't know if anything will," Beth said, "but still it's a nice idea." Then, when he saw her gulping back a yawn, he wondered whether she'd been asleep before he arrived. "I told Henry I can't really do it, though, because pretty soon I'll be too busy. Getting ready for a baby takes time."

A baby.

Right.

He could make time for a baby, Rafe vowed, yanking off his loosened tie. He could do whatever it took to show Beth she mattered.

"But not for eight weeks," he warned, dropping his tie onto the rack. "Remember, the doctor said you've got to get all the medication out of your system."

"I know, but eight weeks is nothing." She slid

back under the sheet, confirming his guilty suspicion that she'd only turned on the lamp for him. "Anyway, there's meat loaf waiting in the kitchen, if you don't mind heating it up this late. I just don't want you wearing yourself out."

But knights never wore themselves out, he reminded himself six hours later as he headed back to the clinic shortly before dawn. It was the mission of protecting other people that kept him strong.

People like Beth, who deserved everything he could give her.

People like Cholo's cousin Billy, who needed someone capable of fighting a legal system that was unfairly stacked against him.

People like Oscar, who had asked if he needed any more repairs around the clinic. Which meant, Rafe suspected, the kid was desperate for some money.

It was lucky, though, because he could use Oscar's help in tracking down everyone at the party where Billy had been spotted with the murder victim. If they could just find a witness before the case went to trial, he'd be in a prime position to prevent another flare-up with the Raptors.

And the sooner he could take care of that, the sooner he could turn all his attention back to Beth.

So he'd arranged to meet the kid early this morning, in order to assemble a list of names and an action plan before the clinic was flooded with other jobs.

"Look," Rafe told him as he unlocked the Legalismo door, "I appreciate your taking the time to help me out." He handed Oscar the ten-dollar bills already folded aside in his pocket, which let them both treat it as a casual transaction, but saw the kid's look of relief as he glanced at the money. "This shouldn't take too long."

"No problem."

There was likely *some* problem, though, or the kid wouldn't be so hungry for cash. Maybe drugs, maybe a shortage at home, and either of those he could deal with. But before calling a social worker, he might as well see what he could find out. Try fishing for clues.

"So," Rafe asked nonchalantly, "who's the girl?"

Oscar shot him a startled glance. "Bianca," he said, and in his voice there was an unmistakable note of reverence. "Her birthday's next week."

"Ah." First guess, and he'd gotten lucky. "Yeah."

"She's..." The kid broke off, as if realizing there was no way of describing Bianca with mere words. "She's great."

All the signs, Rafe realized. This kid was headed for exactly the same kind of mindless, blinding love he'd felt for Rose Moreno at that age.

Before he'd finally learned what could happen if you counted on anyone but yourself.

"You want to take it easy, though, right?" he observed as casually as he could, unlocking the file cabinet with the names of potential witnesses. "I mean, it's not like you'd crash and burn if she ever left."

"She's not leaving." Oscar took his half of the list and picked up a pencil, gesturing to emphasize his point. "Her mom works at the hospital, they're not going anywhere."

There were other ways of leaving, though. People got bored. People got killed.

People got tired of you needing them.

"Yeah, well," Rafe said, spreading out his pages

on the desk between them. One name at a time, one alibi at a time. "Just take it easy, that's all. Things change."

"Sure, I know. Like your wife coming back? Man, that's like something you'd see in a movie."

It probably was. A glorious reunion, complete with soaring music, the camera moving only as far as the bedroom door, then a title filling the screen. Maybe "The End" in triumphant white letters that immediately changed to "The Beginning."

"Right," he said, fingering the medal in his pocket. "New beginning, and all that." Because in a way, it *was* like starting over with a whole new wife.

A wife who understood the importance of his work, even though he'd kept its darker aspects to himself. She had told him so, and he still cherished those memories....

"I should have told you this sooner, but I really admire what you're doing here."

"Just call me. I'll do whatever I can to help."

"Stay as late as you need to. You're making a difference in the world, and that's important."

"She's changed since the accident, you know?" Rafe told Oscar, returning his attention to the list he'd been staring at blindly for too long. "I mean, she really believes in what I'm doing."

Same as when they first met, when she'd been fully supportive of his mission.

When he'd assumed that her design work and his legal clinic would completely occupy the next four or five years before they started a family of their own....

But he could handle a change of plans, all the same.

If she wanted a baby now—and she did—he'd honor her dreams the same way she was honoring his.

"Bianca's the same way," Oscar announced, crossing off a name on his page. "She thinks whatever *I* do is great."

No wonder the kid wanted money, if he had a girl like that to impress. And it was refreshing to hear him excited about something other than Los Lobos for a change. "So what are you doing for her birthday?"

"She likes flowers. I'm gonna get her some first thing in the morning, and she'll think that's it, but then she'll get some more that night. Maybe that afternoon, too, if I work it right. Anyway, a lot of flowers."

A pretty classic statement of love, all right. "Sounds like a plan," Rafe agreed.

A good one, in fact. He might do the same thing for Beth tonight, whether or not he wound up working late—and if he could get Vicente from the Raptors in here, it would be even later than usual.

But just because she appreciated the value of his mission didn't mean he could take her for granted.

No, things were going to be different from now on.

From now on, he'd do whatever it took to make sure she felt loved. Make sure she had everything she wanted. Flowers, a baby, whatever he could offer.

Because he wasn't going to lose her again.

Rafe was going to be late again, Beth discovered when she returned home from the post office with her package from Chicago. Henry was sending everything he could to explain the importance of keeping Dolls-

Like-Me in familiar hands, and it had taken a long time for the clerk to find her shipment.

So she'd missed Rafe's phone call apologizing for the short notice, and urging her not to wait up for him. "You're still not in the best shape of your life, and the extra sleep can't hurt."

Fine.

All right.

She could live with him coming home late, and she'd told him so already.

But six of the past eight nights was disturbing.

Of course, he had explained that with the Lobos and Raptors talking war, the only solution was to negotiate with each gang leader at separate hours…and that right now, he was the only person who could reach them both.

Which was fine. That was important work, no question, and she wasn't going to complain about it. Not when she'd seen through Anne's eyes what a difference Rafe Montoya was making in the world.

Not when she'd seen that look of admiration in Rafe's eyes for the self-sufficient woman he'd thought was Anne.

She could show some of that same independence, Beth knew, and she was doing a pretty good job of it lately. Keeping her mind on the company, at least until they found someone to run things in Chicago. Trying not to spend every free minute waiting for her husband to come home, to start rebuilding the intimacy they'd missed for so long.

But even so, it was taking longer than she'd hoped.

Because you couldn't build much intimacy unless you saw each other during daylight once in a while.

Which she told Rafe the next evening, when he arrived home and placed at the side of her desk the biggest bouquet of roses she'd ever seen.

"This is wonderful, thank you. But I'd rather have *you* than flowers."

"Tomorrow," he promised, moving behind her to kiss the top of her head and letting his hands rest on her shoulders, "I'll be home early. We'll go out, stay home, do whatever you want."

What she wanted was time to enjoy each other. Time to intensify the sharing, the closeness they'd enjoyed the morning she regained her ring.

"Stay home," she answered immediately. "Have dinner together, instead of leaving it in the oven."

He started massaging her shoulders, pressing just hard enough to ease the tension of sitting at a desk. "You sure don't have to cook dinner every night," he said, sounding a little uneasy. "You're already holding down Anne's job *and* designing those new dolls."

"The business stuff is temporary," she reminded him, shifting in her seat so he could work his magic farther down her back. "I've been talking to Henry, and he's trying to line up some interviews for her replacement."

Rafe pressed his thumbs against the tight part of her shoulder muscles, making her sigh. "Just don't sell yourself short. You've got a better head for business than you think."

But he was going on her performance of the past few weeks, not her actual ability. "That wasn't actually *my* head for business," she explained. "I was just doing what I thought Anne would do."

"The name doesn't matter, though. You're still the same person."

Yet she *wasn't* the same person who had drawn admiration from everyone at school for her ability to grasp complexities in a flash. The same person who could make conversation with anyone, anytime, and leave them hungry for more.

The same person who only needed to flash that confident smile to make a man's eyes darken with appreciation.

But even though Rafe had looked at Anne that way, Beth reminded herself hastily, it was herself he made love to. His wife. The woman he wanted to mother his children, the woman to whom he brought flowers, the woman he needed in his life.

Remember that.

She squeezed his hands, then let go and reached for her roses. "Thank you for these. I'm going to put them in that copper-bottom vase, and get your dinner out of the oven."

Rafe stepped back to let her rise, but she saw a troubled expression on his face as they started down the hall to the kitchen. "You know, you really don't have to save dinner for me, especially when I keep getting home so late. I don't need that."

She stopped at the kitchen door, blocking his path with her arms full of flowers. "Rafe, you look after everyone else. You've got to let people look after you, too."

He swallowed. "Well," he said again, "I just…" Then he stopped. Squared his shoulders. And lifted his hands in a gesture of resignation. "Thanks."

All right, at least he understood her point. Maybe

he didn't want anyone fussing over him, but that was part of being married. And he'd said that from now on, he wanted their marriage to be the kind she'd always dreamed of.

Beth deposited her roses on the counter by the sink, freeing her hands in case he needed anything, but he was already taking his dinner plate from the oven. He didn't need waitress service, she decided, so much as the chance for conversation. So... "Tell me about your day."

He set his plate on the table, then reached to open the high cupboard. "First tell me about yours," he said, handing her the vase she'd mentioned and turning to the flatware drawer. "You were gonna have lunch with Deb, right?"

"That was fun," she reported, measuring the height of the roses against the vase. "She's planning a yoga class, so we talked about that. Then after lunch I started the design for a new doll, and I've been doing paperwork ever since. What have *you* been doing?"

Rafe had never been good at sharing the details of his day, but that was before his promise to make things different. Which he honored tonight while she snipped her rose stems, describing his talk with the Raptors leader who insisted that Los Lobos were asking for trouble.

"You can straighten them out, though, right?"

He took a while to answer, and only when she turned from her work at the sink did he mutter, "It's gonna get ugly. I don't want to bring that home."

But his work mattered to her, ugly or not. "I'd be happy to listen!"

"I know." He stood up and moved to the spice shelf where she kept the seasoning, but she suspected it wasn't so much a desire for more pepper as a way of closing the conversation. "Thanks, Beth."

All right, if he didn't want to discuss his most important project, she'd find something else to talk about. Anything to get him into the habit of sharing his life, the way he had with Anne. "What's happening with Oscar?"

Rafe sounded more relaxed as he returned to his seat and shook a miniscule amount of pepper on his stew. "He's all right. Got a new girlfriend."

"Oh, that's sweet." She could imagine the two of them hanging out at Legalismo, chatting about the women in their lives. Although probably more of the chat came from the boy than the man at her table.

Who didn't seem nearly as eager for conversation as she was...

Beth returned to work on her flowers, feeling a curiously familiar heaviness in her chest. "Oscar's like you were at that age, right?"

Another pause. "Kind of, yeah."

Why was this so hard, anyway? "Do you think he talks to *his* girlfriend?"

Rafe didn't even pretend to miss the accusation, which she supposed was his honorable side. But he looked as tense as if she'd just asked him to perform brain surgery. "Beth, what do you want to *know?*"

"Just...what your life is like! It doesn't have to be the clinic, just whatever matters to you."

He rose swiftly and came to her side, grabbing her shoulders and meeting her gaze straight on. "*You* matter."

There was no mistaking the intensity in his body, the passion in his voice. "Then tell me about the best time you had in high school. Or what you used to eat on your birthday." Anything that would build a bridge between them, any story that would entwine his soul with hers. "Tell me when you decided to be a knight in shining armor."

That was a big request, she realized as soon as she spoke, and his uneasy expression reflected the same awareness. "I don't know, exactly," he said slowly, still watching her as he spoke. "I'm not trying to put you off, it's just...I'd have to think about it."

But at least he was willing to try, and that mattered more than the story itself.

"All right," Beth said, feeling the heaviness inside her ease a little, "tell me tomorrow. Will you do that?"

He straightened his posture, and she had the impression of a warrior preparing for battle. "Yes. If you want."

Nobody could mistake such an offer for genuine enthusiasm, but at least if he started talking about things that mattered to him, they would have something to build on. Something to share.

"Okay, then," she agreed, and picked up the vase for her roses. "Tomorrow after work."

"Tomorrow," he said, then leaned forward to confirm the promise with a kiss. "But it's not that great a story. I mean...don't expect too much."

Chapter Eight

Whatever she expected, Rafe vowed as he began quizzing Legalismo's interns the next morning, he was going to deliver.

The story of his life wouldn't be that entertaining, and he'd just as soon Beth never heard the grittier details of his worries and weaknesses, but he could make up for it with enough planning today.

"Most romantic restaurant?" repeated Heidi, who frequently came to work bearing tales of fabulous dinners with her boyfriend. "Like, for an anniversary? Or is it more of an everyday celebration?"

Neither one, he didn't think. "It's just showing my wife she's special."

"You're kind of late to get reservations at Salieri's," Heidi observed. "But maybe you should try anyway. And if you want to make it really romantic, take her shopping this afternoon for something to wear."

Would Beth like that? It was an academic question, since she'd already scheduled her session with Cindy this afternoon, but he filed the possibilities for future consideration.

Dinner at Salieri's. Take her shopping for clothes.

John, the next intern, offered another perspective. "Maybe it's different when you're married," he explained earnestly, "but I don't think women like things to be really traditional. I think you should take her to the dog track, or San Xavier Mission, or something she wouldn't expect."

Greyhound races. Historic churches. At least John got points for creativity.

"Okay," Rafe said. "Anything else you think of, let me know."

He phoned a few other people who offered their own opinions on what sort of evening would show a woman that she mattered, and set himself a noon deadline to make some kind of decision.

Not a play at the arts center, although Beth would probably enjoy that. You couldn't talk during a play, and she seemed to have a passion for talking.

Not a picnic at Sabino Canyon, because while they'd both appreciate the memory of their previous hike and Cindy had said she was in remarkably good shape, the trails probably closed at sunset.

Not dancing, either, because she was usually ready for bed by the time most places got moving.

No, he wanted something romantic. Something unexpected.

"Stay home. Have dinner together."

That wasn't special enough, he knew. It was typical of Beth, trying to put his needs ahead of her own, but he sure didn't want her cooking dinner for him every night. Then leaving his plate in the oven and going to bed disappointed, the way she'd done far too often before the train wreck.

So dinner at home was out of the question.

And dinner at Salieri's was probably out of his price range, no matter how romantic it might be. Beth wouldn't make a scene, but he could imagine the uneasiness on her face when he took out his credit card at a place like that.

Dinner somewhere else, though, would be good. Someplace nontraditional, like John said.

Like the downtown taqueria where they'd had their first date. One afternoon he'd shown up at the homeless shelter on his day off, hoping she might be finishing her shift of volunteer work, and had guessed her departure time almost exactly.

So they'd strolled a few blocks together toward the parking lot where Beth's sorority sisters waited, laughing over her description of today's storytelling kids, and wound up almost at her roommate's car before he worked up the nerve to ask her if she'd like to go out sometime.

"How about right now?" she'd answered immediately, and astonished him by telling her friends to go home without her. "You can give me a ride back, right?"

He had taken her home five hours later, still feeling the same dizziness he remembered from his days of experimenting with every possible high, and reeling under the awareness that this sensation was completely new.

Nobody, not even Rose, had ever affected him like Beth.

Who had listened with wonder as he described his plan to establish a legal clinic for kids who needed someone on their side.

Who had shared her own pleasure in creating dolls for the Down syndrome girls at the center near her home.

Who made him wish, for the first time in years, that he could let himself need someone. That he knew how to keep people with him.

He still wished that.

But things would be different now, Rafe reminded himself. She'd said, that morning when they'd talked about the pro-and-con list, that she wanted to stay with him. He just had to keep her feeling that way, had to remember how much Beth wanted time together.

And dinner at that same taqueria might be a sentimental journey she'd enjoy.

She loved the idea, he discovered when he phoned to suggest dinner at the site of their first date. "Shall I meet you there?" she asked. "We could go by the Fourth Avenue street fair afterwards, because it's one of their big craft nights."

"Sure, let's do that. But I'll pick you up. Like a date, okay?"

She was ready when he swung by the house, wearing the same lacy white blouse he'd admired the other night, and the same great-fitting jeans, as well. "My good luck outfit," she told him as they drove back downtown. "If we're doing Favorite Memories, this belongs on the list."

Not the outfit, he suspected, but what had happened last time she wore it. "Good call. It's sure on mine."

Beth gave him an appreciative smile, and he felt his heart lift. This was working. He could do this.

He could be the kind of man she wanted.

And he held that thought as they shared nachos from his plate and flautas from hers, debated whether the place had changed since their previous visit, and made their way to the street fair where artists' booths lined the sidewalk.

"Pick me out a souvenir," Beth told him, gesturing to a display of ceramic pins that looked like something a kid would make in art class. "Then whenever I see it in my jewelry box, I'll remember tonight."

That didn't sound like she planned to wear it, so he chose a garish sun painted with vivid yellow and red stripes. "This'll show up even from the back," Rafe said, and she laughed.

"Anne would've loved this. Oh, did I tell you her journals came today?"

He remembered her mentioning that someone from Chicago was shipping Anne's things for her to go through at leisure, and wished he could spare her the pain such a task would cause. "You want me to take care of unpacking everything?"

"No, I just put it all in the guest room closet for now. I thought I'd save the journals for reading in a few months, when it won't make me cry."

"Good idea." She'd been crying more often since she recovered her memory, and he knew she was still coping with the belief that somehow she'd failed her sister. That, after a lifetime of being there whenever her twin needed support, she hadn't been nearby when Anne needed her most. He'd better get the conversation back to jewelry, Rafe decided. "How about a moon to go with that sun?"

Beth grinned at him, and he felt a flash of pride that his distraction had worked. "No," she said, "this is fine. Besides, now that we're done with the shopping part, we can just wander. And you can tell me what made you become a knight."

He had hoped she might forget about that, because it wasn't really much of a story. At least not a story that sounded especially heroic, starting out the way it did.

But he'd promised to explain why protecting other people was important, and the only memory he could come up with was almost twenty years old.

Rafe took a long breath. "Okay," he said, moving away from the booth so they could meander through the crowded street. "I'd just moved to my grandfather's house after Aunt Nita took off, so I'm the new kid on the block."

"Wait a minute, how old were you?"

His dad's cousin had left him with Nita when he was seven or eight, he was pretty sure, and he'd stayed with her a few years. "About ten, I guess. Anyway, I'm not too happy about the move—my aunt hadn't been around much, but I was used to her—so I've got kind of a bad attitude to begin with. You come in with a chip on your shoulder, and that's a good way to get beat up."

"Your grandfather beat you?"

She sounded so horrified, he was relieved at having

skipped the part about Nita's boyfriend. "No, never did," Rafe answered, watching the crowd ahead of them to make sure none of the skateboarders veered off course. "I was talking about the gang."

Beth nodded, her eyes sober. "This was the gang you wound up in?"

"Eventually, yeah." A whole separate story, and nothing to do with protecting other people. Or at least not all that often. "But starting out, I was at the bottom of the heap. Except for this one kid, Nardo, who was everybody's punching bag."

"Was he younger than you?"

"Older, actually, but the kind who was easy to pick on." No need to go into details of what people could do to someone weaker, even though she'd probably heard similar stories over the years. "Anyway, I finally said anybody who wanted to pound on Nardo would have to go through me."

"So that's how it started," Beth said softly. "You were sticking up for your friend."

"Well, no." That would've been considerably more heroic, but he couldn't take credit for such a stand. Not if he wanted to stick with the truth. "He wasn't anybody I'd *want* for a friend."

"But you fought for him."

"Not very well." Nobody could fight that many opponents at once, and by the time they'd finished with him he was in no shape to help Nardo. "But the next time it happened, I said the same thing. And the next time, and the next time, and after a while they left him alone."

"But you were still getting beat up?"

"Well, a few more times." Which he regretted,

because the story would sound a lot better if he could omit that part. "*He* wasn't, though, not after I drew the line. The thing is, see, I realized later...looking out for Nardo made *me* stronger."

She was silent for a moment, watching him as they passed a face painter at work. Then she asked, "How?"

"I don't know." He hadn't given the realization much thought, only accepted that protecting people gave him strength. "But it worked. The more I looked out for whoever needed it, the better I could handle everything else. Same thing in detention, same thing in law school, and I guess it's just kind of stayed with me."

Beth smiled at him, and he was surprised at his sense of relief. Maybe this *was* what she wanted from a date, just talking about things he'd never shared with anyone. Nothing too sordid, but there had to be a few more stories he could share.

"And that's why," she said, "you became a knight."

It wasn't a term he would ever apply to himself, but he liked knowing she saw him that way. Knowing she understood the need for someone like him in a world where so many kids had so little protection. "Yeah," Rafe answered. "That's why."

She slid her arm through his, drawing his hand to her lips for a soft kiss. "And you're still doing it."

Every chance he got.

"Yeah," he said again. "Only not so much with the shining armor."

Her laughter warmed him, same as she'd warmed him with her rapt attention during their first visit to the taqueria. "Because you can't bring swords into Legalismo, right?"

"Nobody's ever tried. But I don't think we'd allow any swords."

"Too bad." Still smiling, she turned away from the face painter and started toward the next display. "This is such fun, talking about you."

He wouldn't call it fun, exactly, recalling episodes from his years in L.A. But at least he'd managed to satisfy her demand for a slice of his life, and that should be enough for a while. "Next time," he told her, "it'll be your turn. We haven't talked about you at all."

"That's because I talk most of the time." Then, as they passed another jewelry booth, she regarded him with a thoughtful glance. "You'll get a break this weekend, right? You can tell me more about how you're keeping those gangs from doing a *West Side Story* thing."

He'd just as soon skip that conversation, because the latest negotiations with Vicente and Cholo involved the kind of grim expertise he preferred to keep out of her way. Beth didn't need to hear about the darker parts of his life.

The parts which had never touched her, and never would.

But maybe he would catch a break this weekend. Maybe one of the gang members would risk the threat of retribution in exchange for his offer of protection.

"Well," he hedged, "we'll see how it goes."

She gave him a smile as bright as her new ceramic sun. "Sure," Beth said, and reached for his hand again. "I'm looking forward to it."

* * *

"I'm really looking forward to this weekend," Beth told Karen and Deb while waiting for Lori to return from her third trip to the bathroom. Morning sickness that lasted all day was nothing to envy, but she couldn't help feeling pleased that she might face the same problem within another few months. "Rafe's finally getting the idea that he can share things with me."

Karen, the newest member of their quilting group, shot her a curious glance across Lori's kitchen counter. "What, like his toys?"

It was more like his darker side, the part of him he kept private. "No, like himself. You know, he's always held back from admitting if he feels worried or sad or anything."

"That's just how men are," Deb objected. Beth's college roommate was their only unmarried member, but they'd all agreed her perspective on men was usually the most realistic.

Her perspective on marriage was wrong, though. Because holding back worries or fears was no way to maintain intimacy.

"Not sharing isn't so good," Beth explained, "if you want to have a close relationship."

Lori must have been listening on her way down the hall, because she offered her own opinion as she rejoined them at the breakfast bar. "There are all different kinds of closeness."

"Still, if Rafe's starting to share things with you," Deb offered, "maybe that's proof some men can change."

"Not Jim," Karen said, reaching for the last of the

brownies and then slapping her own hand. "But I figure, if he's got stuff he wants to keep private, that's his business. Not mine."

Didn't she *want* to take care of him? Beth wondered. "You're his wife!"

Karen shrugged, pushing the brownie plate away and refilling her iced tea glass instead. "Sure, but every marriage is different. You're more of a caretaker than I am."

Well, that was true. Taking care of people was her greatest strength, and with Anne no longer needing the weekly pep talk, which energized them both, taking care of Rafe was even more important.

"Beth's more of a caretaker than any of us," Lori observed, picking up her quilt square again, and Deb agreed.

"Good old-fashioned TLC."

"It's just what I've always done." Ever since she could remember, she'd helped Grandma with the meals and Dad with his bouts of loneliness, while Anne contributed in her own way. "Maybe it'd be different if I was an honor-roll kid, but somebody had to take care of the family."

"You're gonna be a great mom," Karen predicted, and Beth felt a rush of happiness in her veins. "I bet Lori's gonna want you to come baby-sit, every chance you get."

"You bet I do," Lori said, smoothing her bunny-printed fabric.

"I can't wait." Taking care of Lori and Eric's baby, due in five months, would be good practice for when she and Rafe welcomed their own. "I'd love to help out."

"Well," Deb told her, "you can help out right now by splitting the last of the brownies with me. I don't want to take home any leftovers."

She'd already eaten more than she should've, especially with dinner still to come. Which reminded her— Beth glanced at her watch and gulped the last of her iced tea.

"I've got to get going," she apologized, picking up her handbag and reflecting once again what a treat it was to use her own roomy purse instead of Anne's tiny one. "Rafe will be home in half an hour."

"That's right," Karen teased, "he's coming home to share his innermost thoughts."

"No, it's not like that!" Although she wouldn't mind if it were, but Karen made it sound like she was trying to take over her husband's life. "It's just, I want him to be able to talk to me."

"I think that's nice," Lori defended her.

It was more than nice, Beth thought as she deposited her glass on the counter. It was the only way of keeping their marriage together. But she couldn't very well explain that to friends who didn't understand the value of a genuine helpmate.

"So," she said instead as she started for the door, "we're meeting at Deb's next time, right?"

"Yes," Deb agreed as Lori waved goodbye and Karen called a farewell suggestion.

"Tell Rafe he'd better appreciate you."

"He does," she called back, hoping that was still true. He was doing a good job of offering all the right gestures, sending flowers every few days and scrupulously thanking her for every little service she took for granted. But they hadn't found time for another in-depth conversation since that night at the street fair.

And that was nearly a week ago.

Tonight, though, he'd promised to be home for dinner. She had started marinating the steak this morning, and all she needed to do before he arrived was make a salad and set the table.

Except that when she got home, there was a phone message from Rafe.

"Beth, I'm sorry, I'm gonna be here most of the night. We've finally got a witness who can make a difference, but this is taking longer than I thought, so don't wait up for me. See you tomorrow."

And that was that.

Well. Fine.

His work was important, yes.

But she couldn't help feeling a stab of betrayal at how energetic he'd sounded. How thrilled at the chance to work late, on behalf of some kids who would never, ever love him the way she did. Some job which, at least for tonight, was giving Rafe all the excitement he needed.

So. Fine. She could work late, too.

She could start on the doll for the new girl at Greenfields, another place that had been delighted to hear about her return. Beth found her latest pattern and started tracing its curves, trying not to think about Rafe.

At all.

Because even though he'd agreed to start a family as soon as her doctor okayed it, she was beginning to suspect he didn't really want the kind of closeness she wanted.

The kind a wife should be able to expect from her husband.

Maybe she was asking too much, Beth admitted as she dug her scissors out of the drawer, but he shared parts of himself with *other* people! Look how he'd opened up to her when he thought she was Anne. He'd been more free with his opinions, more free with his time.

He'd treated her with the same rapt attention everyone paid to Anne Farrell. Starting with that man on the train, who'd lit up the moment she entered the bar car.

And it was fine for Rafe to insist that she was still herself, but in a way it seemed like he had appreciated her twin more than her....

No, that was silly.

She'd gotten over being jealous of her sister a long time ago, when Grandma had pointed out that each of them was special in a different way. No question Anne was better at business, at making people see things her way, at impressing the world with her dazzling combination of intelligence, independence and flair. But Beth was better at nurturing, at making people feel comfortable, at creating a home....

A home where Rafe wasn't spending much time.

If only she could talk to her sister about it! Anne might not grasp why it mattered so much, but at least she would listen. Maybe offer advice or maybe just sympathize, but at least she would *be* there.

At least there would be someone to talk to.

"Anne," she whispered over the tightness in her throat, "I miss you so much."

There wasn't any answer, and she hadn't really expected one. But it would be so sweet to share another conversation with her twin.

To feel like she was in contact with someone she loved.

Instead of feeling more and more alone.

The chime of the doorbell was a relief, because she didn't like where her thoughts were going. Beth found a bored-looking delivery man holding a massive bouquet of tulips, along with a clipboard, and gave him her signature in exchange for the flowers.

Which were probably Rafe's apology.

Gorgeous flowers, she had to admit. But not what she wanted from her husband.

And she might as well tell him so, she realized. Putting his work ahead of his family wasn't the kind of thing a few tulips or roses would change, and she hated to see their budget eaten up by pointless gestures. A weekly floral delivery was the kind of gesture she'd happily accept from a business associate—and probably the kind Rafe would offer if he'd offended some associate.

But this wasn't a business relationship!

So she phoned Legalismo, reaching him on the first try, and plunged into her speech. "Rafe," she said, "the tulips just came. They're gorgeous, but you knew that."

"Ah, good." He sounded both pleased and apologetic. "Just wanted to let you know I'm sorry about not being home."

All right, maybe he was. So was she. Still...

"I appreciate the thought," Beth told him, "but that's not what I want."

A moment's hesitation. "I want to make things right for you."

"You want to make things right for everyone, I know." From the street kids to the clinic interns to his injured sister-in-law to the physical therapist, he treated them all with the same effective blend of charming determination and steadfast command. "But, Rafe, I'm not a…a project. I'm your wife."

"Hey, come on, I know you're not a project."

For some reason, though, she was having a hard time believing him. "The thing is," she said, "I saw more of you when we thought I was Anne than I do now."

He didn't even attempt to deny that. "Yeah, but back then you *needed* more of me. You couldn't even drive, that first week."

"So you kept coming home to play knight in shining armor." A mission which, she realized with a sudden pang of despair, must have been far more enticing than going home to a wife who wanted a relationship of equals. Of people who took care of each other. "Is that what it takes to get you here? Me getting hurt?"

When he spoke again, his voice was tight with what almost sounded like dread. "Beth," he said, "you're not going to—"

"Hurt myself to get your attention?" How could he even think such a thing? "Of course not! You don't really believe I'd try that, do you?"

"No," he answered immediately. "I just think you— I—"

"You'd just rather be at work," she acknowledged, "than here."

For the first time she heard a note of impatience in his response. "I explained this, remember, when we thought you were Anne? You said you understood how important the clinic is."

Which was true. "I know, but—"

"What, you changed your mind?"

His mission was still important, she knew that. But, darn it, so was their marriage.

"What if I did?"

There was a silence. Then Rafe said abruptly, "Look, I can be home in twenty minutes."

It wouldn't help, though. Not when he was only coming in response to a demand.

Not when he wanted to be at the clinic.

"No, never mind." Coming home now wouldn't do any good, and staying at Legalismo might help the kids who needed it. "I know what you're doing is important, I'm not saying that."

"But," he said slowly, as if trying to decipher some kind of code, "you want me to come home anyway."

Somebody might as well get something out of the evening, and it was already too late for her.

"No," she snapped. "I don't."

He sounded even more baffled. "You want me to go on working?"

Why did all the decisions have to fall on her, anyway? "I don't know *what* I want!" Beth cried, and she heard him sigh.

"Well, let me know when you do, okay? I'm trying to make things right, here, but it's not easy."

As if it was easy for her? "It's not like I'm trying

to make things hard,'' she blurted, and reached for the disconnect button.

So she almost missed his dark response. ''It was a hell of a lot easier, though, living with Anne.''

Wrong thing to say, Rafe knew the moment he spoke. He heard Beth catch her breath, then the line went dead. And when he immediately hit the call-home key, there was no answer.

Which shouldn't surprise him. Comparing any woman to another was flat-out stupid, and comparing Beth to her sister was even worse. It *had* been easier living with someone who cheerfully encouraged him to work late, but he should've kept quiet about that.

Now he had to make things right.

''I'll be back,'' he told Frank and Heidi, ''but you guys lock up tonight. Heidi, did you park in the light?''

''I'll walk her to the car,'' Frank said before she could answer, and Rafe decided that was good enough. Normally he'd make a point of striking some balance between practicality and respect for women, but tonight he'd settle for convenience.

Forget everything else.

Just get home.

He covered the twenty minutes in less than eighteen, trying to think of some way to prove Beth mattered far more than Anne. Flowers wouldn't cut it, but what else could he offer?

A baby, he'd already agreed to.

An evening out, he'd tried the other night.

Conversation, sure, but how much conversation could she possibly want? Telling her his life story might take a few hours, maybe even a few days if he remembered every possible moment of pleasure, pain and pride.

But then what?

The lights were still on when he got home, which he hoped was a good sign. At least Beth hadn't gotten so upset she'd walked out, which he could never quite forget was always a possibility.

With her car in the driveway, though, he could dismiss that possibility.

But the reality was even worse.

Because she was huddled on the guest room bed with all the lights off, sobbing her heart out.

Same as he'd found her in the kitchen when she'd tried writing to her sister and wound up in tears.

Only this time the tears were his fault.

"Beth," he blurted, "I'm sorry. I love you more than anyone, and I didn't explain that very well."

She gulped. But when he gently rested his arm around her shoulders, hoping to ease the shaking, she pulled away from him.

"This isn't working," she cried, and he felt his heart twist. "I just keep trying, and I don't know what to do. But I'm not who you want."

"Yes, you are!" No question about that, no need to even consider the possible answers. "You are," Rafe repeated, feeling his throat tighten with an unfamiliar rush of emotion. "My God, I've never loved anyone the way I love you."

"Except Anne."

Oh, hell. Of all the things he could've said on the phone, why had he let slip that revelation about her sister being easier to live with? "No," he protested, "that was *still* you."

But she shook her head, grabbing the pillow and folding it between her arms as she sat up straight, her back against the wall.

With the width of the bed between them.

"It wasn't me," she murmured. "I was just acting like more of a career woman, being more independent, and that's what you really want."

No, that didn't make sense. He'd never fantasized about living with an MBA, with someone who believed in living on parallel tracks.

"If that's what I wanted," he said, jamming his hands into his pockets, "I would've married Anne." No, wait. Bad choice of words. "Or, I mean, somebody like that. I wanted *you.*"

"Anne was easier to live with," Beth reminded him, her voice slightly steadier. At least it didn't sound like she was on the verge of crying again, so maybe he'd helped a little. Or maybe not, because she continued, "And more exciting, remember? There was all this electricity."

"Yeah, I remember it." There had been more than either of them knew what to do with, and he would never forget the rush of learning he could make love to this woman. "But that was *us* making all that electricity."

"The whole time, though, you thought it was Anne."

Which was why he'd resisted that desire with all his strength.

"I didn't know it was you," he agreed, hoping for

the right words as he fingered the medal in his pocket. "Neither of us did. But our hearts knew it, all along."

There was a moment of silence, and he could feel that truth resonating through his soul with a pleasurable warmth. Once in a while, Rafe thought, a revelation could be dusted with magic.

"My heart recognized you," he murmured, and she caught her breath. "*You*, Beth. I never felt like that for Anne, but you… You're who I love."

This time, when he sat down beside her, she didn't back away. But she didn't reach for him, either. Instead, she squeezed the pillow even more tightly against her, looked up at him and asked, "Really?"

Yes, really, but the statement wasn't enough without some action to back it up. "Look," he told her, "I've been trying to figure out how to prove it to you." And the only idea he'd come up with during the drive home was spending more time together. "What do you say we go away for a while? Just the two of us?"

She gazed at him with a cautious expression. "When?"

"Soon as I've got Cholo and Vicente taken care of, we could go anywhere you want." They hadn't taken any vacations together since their honeymoon, although she'd continued visiting Anne on her own. "For a few days, maybe even a week."

Her eyes widened, as if the possibility of a vacation was taking shape in her mind. "You mean it? You'd take time off work?"

"I mean it," Rafe told her. "You matter more." Which she did, and she deserved to know that.

It didn't mean he was depending on her, not with

that same dangerous need he'd felt for his mom or Gramp or Nita or Rose, but Beth was his wife.

He had to put her first.

"We could go to California," she said slowly, letting the pillow collapse in her lap. "I could show you that restaurant Anne and I liked on our last trip. Maybe we could go to the beach, if it's still warm enough, and just...be together."

From the sound of her voice, he couldn't quite tell how she felt about the prospect, and the shortness of breath in his chest disturbed him. He was too close to the edge of need, and he wasn't letting that happen again.

"So," he asked hoarsely, "what do you say to a vacation next month?"

"It sounds wonderful," she answered, and he felt a flicker of relief.

Beth hadn't given up on him.

Now if he could just keep things balanced, keep himself from that old and fruitless dependence, while making sure she felt loved and while keeping Legalismo a beacon of hope....

He could manage that, Rafe vowed. He'd gotten himself out of the Bloods, right? He could do whatever he had to.

"Good," he managed to answer. "Yeah. It will be."

Chapter Nine

It would be wonderful, Beth promised herself the next morning, while searching her desk for the California map on which Anne had marked her favorite hotels.

It would be a wonderful chance to spend time together.

If it ever happened.

But she wasn't going to think that way. She was going to stay optimistic, keep holding on to the hope that Rafe valued their marriage as much as she did.

"You're who I love."

"I never felt like that for Anne."

What more could she want?

"Nothing," she said aloud, wishing she sounded more certain. Rafe was doing everything he could, so she had no business feeling this sense of dread. No business—

Ah. There.

She pulled the map from the drawer, caught by another wave of yearning for her sister when she saw Anne's "two weeks until August!" note scribbled on the front. It was funny, how Rafe had said he couldn't tell their handwriting apart, but probably to a casual observer it would look pretty much the same.

Just gazing at her sister's writing, though, she could see all the other times they'd traded notes in school, sent each other letters from college, addressed birthday cards and postcards and Christmas gifts....

Oh, Anne.

She felt the tears rising in her throat again, and deliberately swallowed them back. Spread out the map on the desk. Reached for a pencil. Right now her job was to think about vacation planning, not to start crying again.

Anne had always done the planning with her usual impressive efficiency, but this was just one more thing Beth would have to learn.

"It's not that hard."

She looked up at the ceiling.

Anne?

Even though nothing looked any different, she could have sworn she heard her sister's voice.

Oh, please...

She'd managed a conversation with her twin in the kitchen once before, when she tried journaling and wound up talking, and maybe she could do that again if she answered the voice in her mind. What had Anne just said?

"It's not that hard."

"You always said that," Beth told her aloud, setting down the pencil and envisioning her sister by her side. "You always said I could run Dolls-Like-Me as well as you could, but I don't know how you did that and planned vacations at the same time."

"Anybody could do it. All you need is a list."

That was typical of Anne, all right, assuming that everyone shared her executive approach to life. Look at how she'd suggested that pro-and-con list on the train.

"You and your lists," Beth retorted. This was exactly like listening to her sister on the phone, and already she felt a sweet familiarity in the combination of annoyance and affection. No matter how bossy Anne could be at times, there was still no one easier to talk to. "Remember what happened when Rafe found that one in my suitcase?"

"At least it got him thinking."

Well, that was true. "I know," she murmured, "it did." He'd been more upset than she could remember ever seeing him, and in a way that was reassuring.

If the very thought of her leaving could hurt him so badly, surely Rafe must love her....

But why couldn't she *feel* it?

She hadn't even asked the question aloud before she heard Anne's answer.

"He said that night, remember, that he'd never been any good at loving."

Right. She remembered that, remembered the anguish in his voice and her own instinct to care for him, reassure him, make him feel better.

"I know," Beth admitted. "He did say that, and it's because his family was so awful, but I know he's trying.'' Sending flowers, promising a baby, giving her everything she wanted...

Except his time.

Except his attention.

Except his heart.

''Aw, Bethie...''

No, she wasn't thinking that way. She was staying optimistic.

"It'll turn out okay," she told her sister, hoping for an immediate confirmation. "I just have to be patient."

Anne was silent.

"Really," Beth said. "Don't you think?"

No reply.

Oh, if only they could talk the way they used to! If only she could get her sister on the phone, talk things through, know there was someone who understood. If only Anne were here, in the very same room, looking at this map with her handwriting on it, suggesting a list of hotels....

Beth felt the pressed-back tears welling up, and realized there was no use pretending that work would provide enough distraction. She *missed* her sister, as fiercely now as ever, and sometimes it seemed like she would never be whole again.

Nobody would ever understand the bond they'd shared, and she couldn't expect them to. Nobody knew Anne the way she did, knew how her twin always had to open the last present, wished you could buy peanut butter "with raisins mixed in," and swore no movie was better than the original *Cinderella*.

No one would ever appreciate how Anne had liked to wear her socks inside out, filed her birthday cards according to color, lent brand-new clothes without hesitation, and never drew a snowman without ears.

How she'd told Brian Ford that Beth deserved better than an ordinary gardenia for prom night. How she talked Grandma into letting them dye Easter eggs in August. How she insisted when they divided their Halloween candy that any leftovers belonged to whoever could identify the donor.

"I didn't say that!"

"Yes, you did," Beth retorted before realizing that her sister hadn't actually spoken aloud. But it was such a relief to hear Anne's voice again, even if only through imagination, that she continued her side of the conversation. "You always knew who gave us what treats."

"But I didn't say that about all the leftovers. It was only the last odd-numbered piece."

Oh, well, maybe. "Even so, you were always better at negotiating." Which was why Anne had been the logical choice to run their company, while Beth continued the original work of designing dolls. "That's why you got the glamorous life."

"That's why you got the family life."

But Anne hadn't wanted a family, any more than Beth had wanted a business.

Had she?

Maybe she had, Beth realized with a twinge of dismay. Maybe both of them had assumed there was no other option than the one they'd been assigned as children, when Grandma tried to make each twin feel special in her own right.

But that would be heartbreaking. If Anne had

wanted a family and felt as though she could never manage it—

"Same as you feel about running the business?"

Beth caught her breath.

But that didn't make sense. Maybe she *was* capable of running a company, same as Anne could have nurtured a family, but that didn't mean she wanted to live in Chicago.

That didn't mean she wanted to put her dreams of a baby on hold.

"It's a whole different thing," she explained. "I might be able to run the business if I worked at it, and I know Henry thinks that'll let him retire sooner, but that's not what I'm best at. I want to matter to a family!"

"You want to matter to Rafe."

More than anything else. But considering how doggedly he avoided her every attempt at nurturing, it seemed like the only way to draw them closer together was by giving him a child.

"Well, and Rafe said he wants a baby," Beth reminded her sister. "So that's going to work out just fine."

"I hope so."

So did she.

Because otherwise...

Better not to think about it. Better to stay optimistic. And she managed to do that for the next few days, squelching every impulse to ask Rafe whether he might take a break sometime and reminding herself that yes, his work was important.

But maybe he sensed her discontent, because on Friday he came home early enough to suggest an afternoon at the street fair. "I've got to meet with the prosecutor at four-thirty, but that still gives us a few hours. Or if there's something else you'd rather do, that's fine."

She had to pick up some fabric samples, but she hated to waste the chance for an afternoon with Rafe. "Would you mind if we just stopped by the mall first?"

They wound up spending the entire afternoon at the mall, wandering from exhibit to exhibit, laughing over which gallery sculpture *not* to take home, and lingering at a display of baby scrapbooks while Beth tried to decide which one might be best for their child. And while Rafe didn't seem to grasp the emotional impact of such a purchase, he told her to take all the time she wanted for browsing.

"Just as long as we don't take anything home today," he warned. "Remember, *I* didn't buy that polar bear sculpture."

"And I know it broke your heart," she teased. "Just watch, someday when you've forgotten all about that, you'll show up at Legalismo on your birthday and there, right in the middle of the lobby, you'll see this bronze polar bear."

He grinned at her, moving to let a cluster of teenage girls examine the celebrity poster display. "It'll be wearing a birthday hat, right?"

Oh, if only this could last. If only they could keep this easy intimacy, this lighthearted enjoyment of one another, she would never wish for anything more.

"Sure it will," Beth promised, swallowing the lump in her throat. "And so will all the interns—I'll get there early and hand out balloons and streamers."

"Good day for me to call in sick," he observed, and she wrinkled her nose at him.

"You've never called in sick a day in your life."

Rafe shrugged, fingering the medal in his pocket. "I don't get sick."

"Why, because of your lucky medal?"

He looked startled for a moment, as if wondering what she meant. Then she saw him make the connection, and he took the medal from his pocket.

"This isn't lucky. It's just something Aunt Nita gave me, a long time ago."

"I think it's nice," she told him, watching the girls move on to the next shop. "I like knowing you have something for…well, if you ever need security."

He took a breath, and she could almost hear his "I don't need any security" protest coming. But he hesitated, glanced at the medal, and then shoved it out of sight.

"So," he said. "Polar bears with party hats. What do you think will happen on *your* birthday?"

Just enjoy the moment, Beth ordered herself. Don't ruin everything by wishing for more afternoons like this, for more fun with Rafe, for more of his time…. "It'll have to be a surprise, remember?"

"Oh, right." But his smile showed a flicker of mischief. "Guess that lets out the leprechaun sculptures, huh?"

"Absolutely," she said, returning her attention to the scrapbook with a page for describing the baby's looks. It was hard to imagine what color hair and eyes their child might have, with hers strawberry-blond and Rafe's so dark. Maybe she'd just have to wait and see. "How much time do we have?"

He glanced at his watch, snapping so swiftly into work mode that she missed the transition, and once again she felt a twinge of regret that he'd brought along his phone. Although except for one call to the clinic, during which she saw the familiar tension returning to his shoulders, he'd made a point of avoiding any Legalismo discussion.

Her husband was trying to make this afternoon special, and she ought to appreciate every moment of it.

Because who knew when it would happen again?

"Almost an hour," he answered now, "because Payton's coming from another meeting. Let's see what else we don't want."

The air-conditioned mall was better for walking than the street fair, and they lingered at every store window that caught their attention. But the best one, Beth saw as soon as they approached it, was the pet shop with four puppies romping together.

"Oh, aren't they darling?"

Rafe glanced from the puppies to her, then gently rested his arm around her shoulders while she stood, watching the gold bundles of fur tumbling in joyous abandon. "Pretty cute," he agreed. "You want to take one home?"

"What, instead of a leprechaun or polar bear?"

"No, seriously."

He sounded serious, she realized, pulling back to look at his face.

Good heavens, he *was* serious.

"A souvenir," he said, "like from our Christmas picnic."

It was a sweet idea, especially since it confirmed that he was enjoying this rare afternoon as much as she was. But he'd forgotten—or else never known—how much work a puppy could be.

"You've never had one, have you?" Beth asked, returning her gaze to the smallest of the litter.

"Well, sort of. Carlos did, when I lived with his family. And my dad's girlfriend." He gestured to the same puppy she had her eye on, then evidently caught sight of the framed pedigree in the window. "Maybe we couldn't afford one of these guys, but we could try someplace else."

"A dog?"

"It's just, you're so good at..." Rafe broke off, apparently at a loss for the right word. "I don't know, it seems like the kind of thing you'd enjoy."

"Nurturing." She felt a chill of uneasiness in her veins. "But pretty soon we'll have a baby to nurture."

"Well, yeah."

He didn't sound disturbed by the prospect, but nor did he sound excited. He sounded neutral, Beth thought, and that was somehow...well, disturbing.

Because the hope of sharing a family was all she had left.

"You still want a baby," she asked carefully, "don't you?"

"Oh, sure." Again the matter-of-fact tone, as if she'd asked whether he still liked ice cream. "But, remember, the doctor wanted to make sure all the chemicals are out of your system first."

All right, maybe he was just being cautious. Not letting himself get too excited until the prospect was at hand.

"But in another six weeks, right?"

"Right." He seemed, suddenly, to recognize the tension in her body, because he drew her closer to him with a reassuring squeeze. "Hey, forget about the puppy. It was just an idea."

Just an idea. "It was a nice thought," she said. "But, Rafe—"

"I know," he interrupted, kissing the top of her head. "We've gotta get moving if I'm gonna make it by four-thirty. Want to head out past the leprechauns, or would you rather see the polar bear one more time?"

He wished he could make Beth smile like that more often, Rafe thought as he drove to his meeting, and again the next morning as she spread the living room floor with the fabric samples she'd picked up yesterday. He needed something to feel good about.

Because for some reason, that discussion at the pet store had rattled him.

Which it shouldn't. He'd known all along that Beth wanted a family, and the sooner the better.

"What do you think?" she asked, and he jerked his attention back to her display for the latest design.

"They're all good." He couldn't quite tell the difference between fabrics that qualified as festive and those considered sedate, but if she wanted his opinion he'd be glad to help. "That green one is nice."

She gave him a rueful smile, as if she recognized how little he could contribute but appreciated his effort, then picked up the pieces.

"Okay, have you got another minute? Because there's one more batch to look at."

He was on the edge of running late already, but

apparently this show of interest mattered to her. And there was no question that Beth mattered more than this morning's staff meeting. "Sure," he agreed.

She hurried down the hall to her office, where she kept stacks of cloth that all looked the same to him, and Rafe heard the phone in the kitchen ring.

Probably Henry, who usually called around this time with his updates on the company, but he picked it up anyway.

"Hello?"

"I've got it," Beth said on the office extension, but Henry interrupted her.

"Rafe, I'm glad you picked up. Because maybe *you* can help me convince Beth to give this some more thought. We really need a strong presence running the show right now, and nobody I've talked to can do as good a job as she can."

"I already said I can't take over," she protested before Rafe could even ask if she'd considered it.

"But you've been doing a great job," the manager persisted, "and it'll be a lot smoother for everyone if the leadership stays in familiar hands. And remember, we can arrange for you to stay in Tucson. Keep working from home, just like you are now, but list your name as the person in charge."

Oh.

Oh, yeah.

With a rush of anticipation, he could see it already. Beth enjoying the excitement and challenge and satisfaction of her work, same as he did. Same as *she* had when they met, before Anne had taken over the business and left her with no outlet for nurturing.

Except himself.

And a family.

Which would be fine, Rafe reminded himself, once he had the clinic so solidly established that a family wouldn't splinter his time and attention. By the end of next year, when he could share his mission with more interns—

"No," he heard Beth answer Henry. "Running the company is more…well, rewarding…than I expected, and in a way I hate to give it up. But Rafe and I are starting a family, and that's going to take every bit of my time."

"Yes, you mentioned that," the manager agreed. "But just for the next year or two, while we look for the right person—"

"I can't wait that long!"

Rafe swallowed. This was Beth's call, he reminded himself, and she had every right to turn down the job. But did she realize what she was doing?

"I'm sorry," she continued, "because I'd like to do this for Anne. I'd feel bad if this meant the end of Dolls-Like-Me. But my family matters more."

He gripped the phone tighter. He *wanted* a wife who put their family first, so why did he feel like a ray of hope had just slipped from his grasp?

"Rafe, any chance you can change her mind?" Henry asked. "I'll keep looking around for someone if I have to, only we all know it'd be better to keep Beth in charge."

It would be vastly better, he knew. Not only for the company, but also for her—because she would finally realize she shared the business ability she'd always credited to Anne. And for him, as well, because if only she had somewhere else to focus her nurturing energy, the next year or two would be far easier on them both.

"It's up to Beth," he told Henry, already wondering what it would take to change her mind. "We'll talk about it, sure, but this is her decision."

"I'm sorry," Beth repeated, sounding as though her decision were already fixed in place. "But someone else will have to take over the company, because that's not what I want right now."

She knew what she wanted, Rafe admitted as he hung up the phone. And of course he was going to make sure everything worked out the way she wanted, whether or not it matched his own preferences.

Because he could do whatever he had to.

He could make time for his family, even while getting Legalismo solid enough that he could take more time off.

But if he could just have another year...

Well, he could at least raise the subject tonight after work. Make a point of getting home in time for dinner.

In fact, make a point of taking her out. And Beth seemed pleased by his offer, suggesting that they visit their favorite pizzeria near the university.

"You know," he told her as they waited for pizza at Terrible Tony's, "Henry had a point about your doing the job for a little while longer. You *could* take over for Anne, anytime you wanted."

"I know. He's been wanting to retire for the past year, and I'd like to fill in while we look for someone else...if only I had the time."

All right, at least she wasn't completely opposed to the idea. At least she hadn't forgotten her original dream of giving Down syndrome girls a better image of themselves.

"I'd be glad to help," Rafe offered. "Because, seriously, you'd do a great job of running the company."

She set down her plastic cup of soda and fixed him with a cautious gaze.

"Not with a baby," she said. "That's a full-time job, right there."

The way she threw herself into nurturing, of course it would be. And he wanted his children to have that kind of mother.

"I know," he said hastily. "You're gonna be the kind of mom everybody wishes they had."

She smiled at the compliment, but there was still a shadow of concern in her eyes. "You said," she reminded him, "you still want a baby."

"Well, sure." More than one, actually, but... "Just, maybe, a little later. I mean, we've got plenty of time."

Beth moved her cup aside and leaned forward to face him across the table, her expression suddenly intense. "You've been saying that for the past year," she told him. "Do you want a baby, or not?"

"I do." Which sounded just like a marriage vow, he realized, and yet it still didn't explain how much he wanted her happiness. "Beth, I want you to have whatever you want."

But such reassurance didn't seem to satisfy her. "That's not the same as wanting to be a father," she said, then picked up her soda and jabbed the straw into the ice before meeting his gaze with a troubled look. "Maybe you've never noticed, but... I don't know, sometimes I feel like I'm in this marriage by myself.''

And, damn it, that was exactly what she'd said on her pro-and-con list. Exactly what he'd been trying to fix, all this time. Hadn't any of his efforts gotten through to her?

''No,'' Rafe protested. ''You're not.''

''Because,'' she continued as though he hadn't even spoken, ''you've already got ten dozen kids at Legalismo.''

Yeah, but that had nothing to do with their marriage. His mission was completely separate from the life he shared with Beth, and why couldn't he explain that?

''I love *you*,'' he pleaded, ''more than them.'' Which was why he wanted to give her everything he could.

She swished her straw through the ice, still without meeting his gaze. ''You keep saying that, but—''

''I mean it.'' Yet how could he prove it, if not with flowers or conversation or spending time together on vacation? ''This is going to work out,'' he promised, but for the first time he felt a tremor of doubt.

What else could he try?

What more could he *do?*

And maybe Beth shared his doubt, because when she moved aside her cup as the waiter arrived with their pizza, she looked at him with an expression so forlorn that his heart twisted in his chest. ''Well,'' she said softly, ''I guess we'll see.''

She wasn't giving up on him, was she?

No, she couldn't.

She couldn't.

But she'd already made that list of reasons to leave him....

"This is going to work out," he repeated, only this time he said it to himself. Making promises to Beth might not do any good, and he wasn't going to make promises he couldn't keep.

He was, however, going to do whatever it took to make things right.

Whatever it took to set the world straight.

Whatever it took to stay strong.

Like protecting whoever needed someone on their side...which, right now, was everyone who'd suffer if the Lobos and Raptors made good on their threats of war. The kids in the wrong place during the inevitable drive-by shootings. The parents grieving over lost sons. The teenage girls whose babies would grow up fatherless.

Preventing a war, at least, was a mission he could deal with. And as a side benefit, if he managed to get both Vicente and Cholo to agree on backing off, Legalismo would command a significantly higher level of respect on the streets.

Which meant more opportunity for making a difference. More chance for the kind of grant money it would take to add new staff people, leaving him time for a family with Beth....

Who wasn't giving up on him. Not yet.

He could still make things right.

He just had to keep trying.

He had to be working harder than ever, Beth decided, even though he made it a point to phone home every few hours. Always with the reassurance that he loved her, that things would slow down soon, that all he needed was another session with some gang leader.

Or some kid in trouble.

Any kid.

And it seemed like there were hundreds of them.

Which was why she'd found herself grinding her teeth lately, to the point where Cindy commented on it during one of their sessions.

"Seems like you're more stressed out *now* than when you thought you were Anne."

"It's just Rafe's job," she explained, making a conscious effort to relax her jaw. She wasn't even going to mention her calendar showing only five more weeks before they could try to conceive. She couldn't in any conscience suggest a baby just yet. "Things are really tense at the clinic right now."

"That's the trouble with his kind of work," Cindy agreed. "You get people coming at you from all sides, and then it's hard knowing what to do first."

Not for Rafe, though. He seemed exhilarated by the challenge of preventing an all-out war, which would let him prove Legalismo could be trusted.

Not for her, either, because she had to do *some*-thing with her time. And at least searching for Anne's replacement while Henry delayed his retirement, even though in a way she regretted not taking the job herself, gave her a sense of doing some good in the world.

Because Rafe sure wasn't letting her do anything for him.

"I know," Beth muttered, and gritted her teeth again.

He wasn't even letting her share his workload by

listening to stories about his day. Last night she'd set the alarm clock for midnight, guessing when he might be arriving home and ready to talk, but after waiting for an hour she'd given up and gone back to sleep.

"Think relaxing thoughts," Cindy ordered. "Remember, you're still recovering, and you need to take care of yourself. Make sure you have time for easy things like watching TV."

So that night, after once again setting the alarm for midnight and then changing her mind—after all, what was the point?—she settled down in the living room to watch a rerun of *Gone With The Wind.*

Scarlett had just thrown the vase at Rhett when the phone rang, and she was relieved to see the screen give way to a commercial as she picked it up.

"Anne," came a vaguely familiar voice, "this is Greg."

She'd gotten a few calls from people who had known her sister, but she couldn't remember anyone named Greg.

"Remember," he continued, "we met at the coffeehouse, the night of the poetry reading? I just got back from two weeks in New York, and I thought about you the whole time."

Oh, that was nice. And in a way she hated to disappoint him, but it wouldn't be fair to let him think he'd phoned a single woman.

So. One more time with the explanation she'd memorized over the past few weeks.

"Greg," she began, "I'm sorry. There was a mistake, but I'm not Anne."

"Really? You sound a lot like her," he said easily. "Anyway, is she home?"

"Uh, no." In a way she regretted it, because she remembered Greg as the type of man she might have enjoyed. "I mean…when I told you I was Anne, that was wrong. I'm actually Beth, okay?"

"Okay, well, Beth's a nice name." He sounded so matter-of-fact, as if it were a simple case of nickname preference, that she realized he still thought he had the right woman. "Anyway, you want to go for coffee?"

There was no point in explaining, Beth decided, the whole mistaken-identity story, much less that she'd been seeking distraction from a man she couldn't let herself want. Better to just refuse before the movie started again. "No, I can't. Thanks, anyway."

"You sure? I'd really like to see you again."

It was flattering, she had to admit. And she couldn't help feeling a flicker of temptation, considering Rafe's show of jealousy when she'd come home with her description of flirting at the coffeehouse.

But repeating such an action now would be unforgivable.

"The thing is," she said, "I'm married."

A momentary silence. "Were you married the other night at the coffeehouse?"

All right, maybe she'd better explain the whole story. "Yes, but—"

"Okay," he interrupted cheerfully, "so if you're going around giving out your phone number, am I right in thinking your marriage isn't that big a deal?"

For a moment she found herself stunned with the accuracy of his glib assessment, which was far too close for comfort.

"It's, uh…"

"Look, I don't want to get you in trouble," he said, evidently taking her hesitation as a sign of distress. Which it was, but not the kind he must be expecting. "Is your husband there breathing down your neck?"

"No." Maybe he would be breathing down her neck if he were at home, but she couldn't remember the last time he'd come home early and stayed.

And that hurt.

"So either he's out working and doesn't care what he's missing—"

Which, again, was painfully close to the truth, and which made her wonder how Rafe would react if he came home from work and found her off with some other man. Because in a way, it would serve him right.

"Or he's out playing," Greg concluded, "and you should be doing the same thing."

But that wouldn't solve anything, and the fact that she'd even thought of such a betrayal was appalling.

"I can't," she said hastily.

"You were doing a pretty good job of it the other night."

Coming on top of her own guilty awareness, the comment stung. "I didn't know who I was!" Beth protested.

"Hey, now you've really got me intrigued." He sounded even more fascinated than she'd felt watching Scarlett and Rhett. "Let's go get a cup of coffee, that same place, and you can tell me about it. Life stories, what do you say?"

Why, *why* couldn't Rafe be so eager to share life stories?

"I can't," she repeated, closing her eyes. What was

she doing, secretly resenting her husband to the point where she could even consider going out to meet someone else?

This wasn't fair to either of them. Not Rafe, not herself.

For that matter, not even Greg.

"Even if your husband's out working?" he persisted. "I tell you, Beth, the guy doesn't know what he's missing."

But all he was missing was a wife who nagged for stories about his day, who couldn't live up to her sister's gift for detachment....

"Somebody like you," Greg continued, "the way you listen—"

"He hates that!" she blurted. "I'm always trying to get him to talk, and he doesn't want to."

A situation which, she had to admit now that she was facing the stark truth, was probably as tough on him as it was on her. And which, she knew with a sudden hollowness in her chest, was never going to change.

No matter how much she wanted Rafe's full attention on their family, no matter how hard she tried to be the kind of woman with whom he'd love to share every detail of his life, she might as well be wishing for the moon.

"He never will," she concluded, and felt startled at how intensely the flash of anger raced through her skin. Where had that been hiding all this time?

Greg must have heard the frustration in her voice, because he immediately answered with his own pitch. "Yeah, see? So what do you say? Want me to come pick you up?"

"Oh, no. No, I can't." She wanted intimacy, yes, but she wanted it with Rafe. And she wasn't going to get it. "No."

"Three 'no's, huh?" He sounded rueful. "Not so good."

Not so good, no. But none of this was Greg's fault, and she owed him at least that much of an explanation.

"It's not you," Beth told him. "It's me." Because with all this resentment rising inside her, all this growing awareness that her hopes for change were a complete waste of time, she wasn't the kind of woman anybody could enjoy right now. "I'd be terrible company."

"Ah."

"I don't like who I'm turning into," she blurted. Setting the alarm clock for midnight? Viewing a baby as their only hope? Trying to make her husband talk, trying to change the kind of person he was, and resenting the street kids who needed him? "I'm getting way too clingy, and that's—" Oh, good heavens, now she was unloading her troubles on a perfect stranger. "I'm sorry, that's not your problem."

But Greg's voice was curiously sympathetic. "Sounds like," he agreed, "you've got more than your share."

"Well, that's what happens," she muttered, "when your husband is trying to save the world." A quest that had sounded fine before their marriage, which still sounded fine in theory, but she was only now beginning to realize its true cost. "And as long as he's doing that, he can't give me what I want."

Maybe this man was a psychologist or something,

because he still sounded interested. "And you want...?"

A family, of course, but their marriage was in no shape for a baby. "Somebody," she said slowly, "who doesn't always have to be a knight in shining armor. Somebody who'll come home and let me take care of *him* once in a while!" But she already knew that dream was impossible. "And that's never going to happen."

"Doesn't sound like it," Greg agreed, then the persuasive note returned to his voice. "Sounds to me like you need to get your mind off things for a while, come have some fun."

"No." She was clear on that much, anyway, and somehow that certainty made everything else feel clearer. "What I need is to quit waiting for him to change." With frightening speed, the rest of the pieces tumbled into place. "Because our marriage is never going to change," Beth concluded, and reached to hang up the phone. "Rafe's never going to do anything different, and that means... That means I have to."

Chapter Ten

"I have to go to Chicago," Beth announced, and Rafe felt his bones lurch. When she'd arrived at his office shortly after the interns, his first thought had been that she wanted to summon him home for breakfast, the way she'd done last time he worked through the night.

But he'd never expected an announcement like this. "You...what?"

He probably didn't sound too steady, and when he moved to close the door behind her he didn't feel too steady, either. Lack of sleep, maybe, but somehow Beth's expression confirmed it was more than that.

"I have to go to Chicago, and start focusing on the business. Last night," she said, sitting down in the chair by his desk—damn it, he should've gotten a sofa in here—"I got a call from this guy who thought I was Anne."

Just keep her talking. Just let her talk, and figure out how to make things right.

"Okay," Rafe said, dragging his desk chair closer to hers. He sure didn't need a piece of furniture between them, not if she was talking about Chicago.

"He wanted me to go out with him, just coffee, only it probably would've turned into more. So I told him I was married, and that was that."

So far, so good. But that didn't explain the look of rueful determination in her eyes, nor the chill of uneasiness under his skin.

"But the thing is," Beth continued, looking just beyond him at the wall of abandoned baseball caps, "I actually found myself thinking about it. Thinking about how you'd feel if I did that—"

Like someone had jabbed a knife into his heart.

Then jerked it sideways.

"And I realized, that was awful of me. I've been resenting you, a lot more than I knew."

And dragged it down through his guts.

"I should've come home," he managed to say. Even at four in the morning, he should have left the clinic long enough to at least wake up with her. "Beth, I'm sorry."

"I know," she said softly, turning her gaze to his. "So am I. Because this isn't all your fault."

So it was *her* fault? What was she saying, she'd *been* with that other man? He felt a jolt of panic burning in the wake of the knife before realizing she couldn't have, she wouldn't have.

Not Beth.

"What—"

"*I'm* the one," she concluded, "who needs to

change. If I'm going around thinking about ways to hurt you, there's something wrong with me.''

"But you didn't hurt me," he managed to protest. Not Beth. Please. "You didn't do anything."

"No, I didn't." *Thank you, God.* "Not last night. But I spent most of the night thinking it over, talking to Deb and Lori and finally even to Anne, and that's when I realized how bad things have gotten."

How bad...

No.

He could fix things.

He could do whatever he had to.

But for some reason he couldn't seem to draw a breath.

"Don't you see?" Beth asked, leaning forward and holding him fast, holding him helpless, with her gaze. "I'm hurting both of us, expecting you to be somebody you're not. You've been a knight your whole life, and I keep waiting for you to give that up...to make me feel important, fill all the holes in my life. And that's not fair to either of us."

"A knight your whole life."

Just take a breath.

"Not fair to either of us."

Breathe.

Say something.

"I thought you wanted a knight."

"So did I," she said. Then, standing up, she moved behind him and laid her hands on his shoulders. "But I'm asking too much. You're trying to give me everything, and give the clinic everything, and you can't do it."

Yes, he could.

He could do whatever he had to. Rafe jerked away from her touch, hastily rising and turning to pull her into his arms.

"Beth, I love you."

She still felt so right against him, still fit into his embrace with the same sweet warmth as always. But when she looked up at him, he saw the shimmer of tears in her eyes.

"I love you, too," she murmured, "and that's why I've got to leave. Because you're not getting what you want, any more than I am."

But what he wanted was her. He couldn't let her walk out, take off for Chicago, and yet he already knew in the oldest part of his soul that you couldn't keep someone who wanted to leave you....

"You'll get what you want," he promised desperately. "A year from now, you'll be holding our baby."

But she shook her head even as he delivered the pledge, leaving him even more off balance than before. "It's not just a baby, don't you see? I want to be special!"

"You are!" Damn it, why couldn't he make her see that? "Beth, you are."

"Not really," she said, and he was startled by the bleak certainty of her voice, as if she'd already thought through every possible angle and come to a stark conclusion. And that impression was reinforced when she pulled back from him, retreated to the edge of his desk, crossed her arms and met his gaze. "You don't need me."

Of course not, but he loved her. Wanted her.

Fiercely, forever, with an intensity that sometimes frightened him. "I—"

"You don't need anyone," she continued. But that was only practical, a matter of survival. That had nothing to do with love. "And the thing is," Beth said, still watching him across the endless distance between them, "I haven't been fair to you. I've been asking too much ever since we've been married, expecting you to make me into someone important."

"You're important to me," he protested, knowing even as he spoke that she might not believe him, might not accept it. For some reason he couldn't seem to get through to her, make her realize how much she mattered.

How very, very much.

And his suspicion was confirmed when she blinked back what looked like another teardrop and turned to pick up her purse.

"Not enough," she said shakily. "It won't ever be enough, and that's why I have to find some other way. I need to take over for Henry, and I need to spend more time with the Down syndrome girls."

Begging had never worked. Bargaining had never worked. But, God, she was starting toward the door.

She was leaving him.

For a bunch of Down syndrome girls...

"They're why I started making dolls, remember?" Her voice sounded like it was coming from somewhere far away, even though she was still right there in his office. "Those girls at Greenfields loved having look-alikes, and then Anne took over the marketing, and that was fine. But I can do more of that, matter to people, if I get more involved with the business."

The business. "In Chicago," he said numbly.

"Well, that's where they need someone running things." She was leaving him. Right now. Right here. "I'm not saying this is permanent," she continued with that same quaver in her voice, and he felt another crack behind his ribs. "But for now…Anne's apartment is still empty, so I can stay there."

Breathe.

Say something.

"Beth…" he choked, and saw the tears spill over as she cried out in despair.

"This is the only way! If I stay here, we're both going to keep trying and failing and hurting each other, and I can't keep doing that."

God, was she hurting like he was?

Because if there was any way he could save her—

Rafe closed his eyes, hoping he'd guessed wrong.

And knowing, even as the recognition knotted what was left of his guts, that he hadn't.

"You're saying," he managed to ask, "if I love you, I'll let you go to Chicago?"

Without even attempting to wipe away the tears on her face, she nodded. "The kind of person you are… Rafe, I think that's all you *can* do."

All he could do.

Letting Beth go.

People leave.

Not Beth.

Not again.

No.

I can't do it.

You can do anything you have to.

"Okay," he said, hoping his voice sounded steady.

Hoping he could still, somehow, make things right. "So you're going to Chicago for a while. What can I do to help?"

His help was everything she could ask for, Beth reminded herself a week later as the checklist on her desk grew shorter and shorter.

So why did she feel so forsaken?

He was only doing what she'd asked. Letting her go for as long as she wanted, giving her the chance to build a life where she could matter to someone.

Oh, but if only she could matter to him...

"They'll turn on the utilities tomorrow," Rafe reported, hanging up the phone and crossing off another note from the list. "I guess Anne told you about Chicago winters, but that's still a few months away."

Even though his voice carried no sign of a question, she knew what he meant.

Because she'd wondered the same thing every hour for the past week.

"I don't know how long I'll be there," she told him, taping shut another file box.

"You said that." He took an address label off the desk and, with a savage slam, smacked it onto her sealed carton. "What's next?"

All she had left on the checklist was running these boxes to the post office, cleaning the desk, and ironing her clothes for tomorrow. But the way he sounded, Rafe could probably use a break. "You've been working thirty hours already," Beth offered. "You don't have to do any more."

"Yeah, I do," he said flatly, turning to the last

flattened box and jerking it into shape. "You're still my wife."

And yet that wasn't enough.

Still, no matter how long she stayed in Chicago, she wasn't about to remove her wedding ring. Once had been bad enough, and she didn't need that heartache on top of everything else.

Although she had no business feeling sorry for herself, Beth knew, when Rafe—for all his deliberate calm—was probably hurting every bit as much as she was.

"Things will be better this way," she reminded them both, and he shot her a dark glance over the top of his box.

"What do you want me to say?"

Say you love me.

But he'd said that already, over and over, and it wasn't what she needed.

He couldn't *give* her what she needed, the satisfaction of mattering...and with all her demands for his limited time and attention, she was no better for him.

"Say you understand," Beth pleaded. "Neither of us can change enough to be what each other needs."

"Maybe not."

His voice was so quiet that she felt her heart thud. For the first time, he was actually agreeing with her.

And even though that shouldn't hurt, it did.

With her hands shaking, she gathered up her earliest designs. These had to come with her. She had to hold on to whatever she could, and she couldn't hold on to Rafe.

Who was silently taping the sides of the cardboard box into position for her to load the remaining folders.

But even though she couldn't hold on to him, she had to leave him with something. Some sense of appreciation, acknowledgment, forgiveness, grace...even simple friendship. Beth cleared her throat.

"I really admire what you're doing for those kids at the clinic."

He yanked off another strip of tape.

Lined it up against a rough edge.

Smoothed it into place.

Picked up the tape again.

Yanked off another strip.

All with the same stark detachment he'd shown ever since she explained why she had to leave.

"It'll be better this way," she repeated.

He smacked the tape against the final side of the box. Then fixed her with a dark gaze.

"Who are you trying to convince?"

"Both of us!" It had to be better, because how could it be any worse than this? Still loving him, still knowing she would never matter to him, and knowing neither one of them could change. Staying would only mean hurting them both, but leaving was almost too painful to endure. "Rafe," she pleaded, "this is *hard.*"

He set down the finished box and faced her across the length of the desk. "Then stay."

If only he meant it.

If only she could.

But she knew what would happen. She'd been watching it happen for the past six months.

"And make us both miserable?" she reminded him. "Because that's what we've been doing, ever since the train trip." Although actually it had started long before her vacation, which was when she'd finally made that pro-and-con list. When she'd finally admitted their marriage was in trouble. "Before that, even."

His jaw tightened. "Not all the time."

"Not all the time, no." There had been the joy of the night they'd discovered who she was, and the pleasure of their taqueria date, and only last week the fun of picking out sculptures...followed by that sobering moment at the pet store. "But it's like we got a second chance, and even then, we still couldn't be what each other needed."

He closed his eyes for a moment, and she could almost see him recalling the failures. The nights she'd waited up for him, only to find he couldn't talk about his day. The times he'd phoned home to check in, only to find her asking for more time than he had to give. His crusade. Her yearning. His passion. Her dream.

"We're not right for each other," Beth concluded, and he met her gaze with a new heaviness on his face.

Then, very softly, he answered, "I know."

Oh.

It surprised her how much the acknowledgment hurt. Almost as if he'd severed her last hope, her last fantasy of a magical happy ending.

But what had she expected, anyway?

They didn't belong together, and all they could do was admit it. Acknowledge it. Deal with it.

So she picked up the rest of her patterns and deposited them into the box he'd given her, then reached for the last address label.

"This way," she said as brightly as she could manage, "the Legalismo kids can have your full attention, and I can try do more for the girls who need to feel special." Try to be more like Anne, try to take pride in her business rather than her frustrated hope for a family. "This is a good thing."

Rafe took the label from her, slowly smoothed it onto the box, then hefted it and the other two in his arms.

"Maybe if we both keep saying that," he told her, "it'll sink in."

Then, without even a glance in her direction, he walked out.

Leaving her alone in the office.

Trying not to cry, because that wouldn't help anything.

Just keep going.

Let Rafe take the boxes to the car, let him drive all the way to the post office alone.

Just don't start crying.

This was better for them both, Beth reminded herself as she swept the dust fragments off the top of the desk.

This way, she wouldn't throw herself at him and beg for another try.

They'd tried. Over and over, and they couldn't change who they were.

So she needed to focus on something else.

Chicago, she decided, surveying the empty bookshelves. Think about Chicago.

About the city she'd enjoyed touring with her sister.

Yes, Anne would be safe to think about. Because

while that aching sense of loss still hadn't faded, at least Anne was separate from this marriage. In fact, Beth decided, maybe the best thing she could do right now would be to sit down with her sister's journals.

She'd saved the latest in her carry-on bag to read during the flight tomorrow, but she needed Anne with her now. So she retrieved the leather-bound journal and settled down on the bed where she'd slept as Anne Farrell.

Whose first entry sounded so much like her sister's voice that Beth found herself caught between laughter and tears.

"Taking off at five in the morning, after I swore I'd never do that again. But what did I expect, Donald Duck?"

Oh, this sounded exactly like Anne. Planning a board meeting, annoyed by her increasingly noisy neighbor upstairs, wondering whether to send Marc a rose.

A manicure after work. Lunch with Henry. Renew the health club membership.

Cancel the book group. Shopping for shoes.

Anniversary present for Beth and Rafe. Two years already, and who would've thought?

Thought what?

She fumbled to turn the page where her sister's writing continued. "I'm worried," she read, "about Bethie. She keeps saying Rafe is so busy with the clinic, he doesn't need her. But she's always felt like she's no good unless somebody needs her."

No, that wasn't true.

"And Rafe's not the type who needs anybody, I don't think. He sounds pretty independent."

Yes, but she could be independent, too. She would have to be.

After all, she was going to Chicago on her own. She was going to run a business.

"I can be as independent as anyone else," Beth said aloud. As self-sufficient as Anne, as detached as Rafe...who had never once tried to talk her into staying. "I can be as independent as he can."

Hearing the words made her feel more capable, and she firmly closed the journal so she could talk to her twin without any distraction.

"In another few months," she announced, "I'm going to have a whole new life where people *will* need me. Rafe will be fine without me, and I won't be hurting over him anymore. You'll see."

No response from her sister.

"You'll see," Beth repeated. "In another few months, I'll have him out of my system."

She would, of course. She would no longer wake up hurting.

She would be an independent woman, who didn't yearn or worry or even *care* about Rafe Montoya.

Except, somehow, the prospect of that hurt even worse.

He wasn't hurting.

He was fine.

He could mail these packages, head home through rush-hour traffic and spend one last evening with Beth, all without breaking a sweat.

Rafe glanced at the Now Serving # sign above the post office counter, wondering how long it would take them to get from fifty-eight to seventy-three.

But there was no hurry. It wasn't like he had any more errands.

It wasn't like Beth wanted him home.

"Number fifty-nine," called the clerk, and a woman with dozens of envelopes shuffled to the counter.

This was going to be a long wait.

Rafe set down his boxes and leaned against the wall, fingering the medal in his pocket.

Which he'd found himself doing more often lately, even though it meant hearing Beth's comment in his memory.

"I like knowing you have something for...well, if you ever need security."

She had it wrong, though. He didn't need anything.

The medal was just a habit.

A stupid one, probably, because a medal couldn't change anything, couldn't make you stronger. No, strength came from protecting other people.

From looking out for people who needed it. People who were hurting.

People like Beth.

She kept insisting everything would be fine, that she could take care of herself in Chicago, and so far he'd managed to take her word for that. But in spite of her determination to change her life, to keep the business going the way Anne had envisioned, she was having a hard time sleeping.

A hard time packing her things.

A hard time getting ready to leave, because she'd already admitted that tomorrow morning was going to be difficult.

"Number sixty, over here."

She had asked him not to drive her to the airport, explaining that she'd rather keep things simple and insisting that he treat the morning like any other workday.

So he'd agreed, knowing Beth needed all the support he could give her.

Even if it meant letting her go without a fanfare.

Even if it meant letting her go...

Because it wasn't like he had any choice. He'd tried to stop his mother from leaving—all these years later, he could still hear those desperate pleas of "Mommy, don't go!"—and it hadn't worked. He'd needed his dad, then Aunt Nita, and that hadn't done any good. He'd tried to save Gramp and Carlos, and failed again. And by the time he'd failed to keep Rose with him, he'd realized how futile such efforts were.

You couldn't keep people from leaving you.

No matter how much it hurt to lose them.

"Number sixty-one."

All he had to do, Rafe knew, was concentrate on strength. On taking care of whoever needed it. There, the kid waiting for his mom, looking as restless and bored as only a ten-year-old surrounded by grownups could look.

Go talk to him.

And when the kid's mom finished her errands, to the tired-looking grandmother who probably needed a listening ear.

That worked until number seventy-two, at which point the grandmother moved to the counter, and he found himself once again fingering the medal in his pocket.

Nothing he needed, of course. Nothing he depended on.

Hell, he could get rid of it right now if he wanted. He could give it to that guy sweeping the floor. Guy looked like he could use a break, a clap on the back, and—

"Number seventy-three."

Ah. Never mind. Rafe took his boxes to the counter and saw the janitor leave before he finished his mission. Still, he *could* have gotten rid of the medal, just like that.

Because he didn't need anything, except maybe some people to take care of when things got tough.

So. What else could he do for Beth?

With the packages safely off to Chicago, about all he could do was to make her last night at home as easy as possible.

No flowers. No fireworks. He already knew she didn't want any fuss.

But bringing home some kind of take-out dinner might be good. Nothing from the taqueria, nothing sentimental, but a box of chicken ought to be fine.

And it was, he saw when he got home and set down dinner on the kitchen table, because Beth looked surprised and pleased.

"I just thought," he said as casually as possible, trying to forget this would be their last dinner, "you shouldn't have to worry about cooking."

"Oh, Rafe." She picked up a handful of napkins and kissed him, same as if this were an ordinary night and he'd done her some ordinary favor. Except her eyes held a glimmer of sadness, and she gave him a worried glance as she spread out the napkins.

"You're going to eat right when I'm in Chicago, aren't you?"

He hadn't even thought about it, but he would do whatever he had to. "Don't worry about me."

Beth took a serving spoon from the drawer and set it beside the coleslaw. "I'd promise not to," she said wryly, "but I bet you'll be worrying about me, too."

Something else he'd just as soon not think about. "Yeah," he admitted. "Right now, though, I'm just worried the chicken will get cold."

She actually smiled at that, and he felt a flicker of pride. Which grew stronger, more pleasurable, as they made it all the way through dinner with remarkably easy conversation. And when he actually made her laugh with his description of the kid in the post office, Rafe felt the glow throughout his entire body.

He could still make her happy.

One way or another, he could still take care of the woman he loved.

She seemed as glad as he was to linger at the kitchen table, but finally seemed to realize they'd been sitting for nearly an hour with the remains of dinner on the table between them, because she took a deep breath and then stood up.

"This was nice," she told him, and picked up both their plates. "Thank you."

All right, time to return to the business of everyday life. Rafe dropped the chicken box into the trash. "You're all set for tomorrow?"

She nodded. "How about you?"

The question startled him, making him wonder for one burning moment how someone who cared that much could just walk out. But it happened all the time, he should know that by now, and he managed to answer matter-of-factly as she took their dishes to the sink, "I've got a meeting with Oscar and Cholo, first thing."

"You'll probably leave before I do," Beth observed.

"That's how you wanted it, right?" This morning he'd listened to her phoning for the shuttle pickup, while clenching his fists in his pockets—and damn it, the medal he didn't need was still there. "Because I could see them later, take you to the airport if you want."

"No, it's better this way." She turned on the water without quite meeting his gaze. "I'd rather not do the whole goodbye thing, and leave you waiting around... I'd rather do it like when Anne and I would go on vacation, and we'd just say goodbye the night before."

They had never made a big production of vacation goodbyes, and he'd always accepted that. But suddenly the idea of saying goodbye the night before made his heart cramp.

"That's tonight," Rafe said.

She shot him a curious glance, as if she'd heard something unexpected in his tone. "Yes."

God, why was he hurting all of a sudden? He was fine, he could do whatever he had to, but for some reason he hadn't expected it to hurt this much.

"I don't want to say goodbye," he blurted.

She reached for the soap, with a smile that struck him as carefully cheerful. "Well," she said in a reassuring voice, "it's not forever! We'll see each other again."

But it might as well be forever. She might promise to return, same as his dad and Aunt Nita and Rose had promised, but by now he knew better than to believe it. It had taken him almost two years to wave her off on those Sisters Vacations without bracing himself for the forthcoming loss, and look what'd happened on the train trip.

"That's what I thought," he muttered, "last time you left."

That sobered her, as well, because he could see her face grow more serious. But she reminded him, "We *did* see each other again. We just didn't know it at first."

And they'd wasted nearly a month while they thought Beth was dead...a loss he couldn't imagine enduring again.

He couldn't do it.

He could watch her leave for Chicago if that's what would make her happy, but—

"Don't die," Rafe said.

The passion in his voice must have reached her, because she rested her hands on his shoulders and looked at him with concern in her eyes.

"Don't you, either," she warned. "*You're* the one people shoot at."

"Yeah, but I can take care of myself."

With a soft sigh, Beth took a step back. "And me," she said ruefully, "and Oscar, and everybody else. But you don't let anyone take care of you, and—" Then she broke off. "Never mind. I should get this cleaned up."

The kitchen looked fine, but he could understand her wanting to change the subject. This wasn't the kind of conversation for a comfortable evening at home.

"Leave everything in perfect shape, huh?" he managed to ask, then realized there was nothing left to do except put plates in the dishwasher. "There isn't much."

She glanced at the tabletop, then wrung out her soapy sponge again. "I have to do *some*thing."

Yeah, probably so, because she sounded almost as edgy as he felt. Which was no way to prepare for a flight to Chicago. "You have to get some rest," he protested. "You've got a big trip tomorrow."

"I know." She ran the sponge over the tabletop, pressing so hard her knuckles looked white. "I know."

Scrubbing the table wasn't going to take the edge off her nerves, either, Rafe knew. But if it was just a question of getting her to relax, he'd learned how to do that the first month they met. "Let me help," he told her. "Let me give you a back rub."

She looked up from the table, her expression a mixture of caution and shyness. "What kind?"

So she remembered as clearly as he did how often the back rubs had turned into something more. And she evidently had the same doubts about ending their life together with a memory that would leave them yearning for more. "Whatever kind you want."

Beth hesitated, as if trying to weigh her options. "Just…"

"Come on," he ordered. A shoulder massage was at least something he could give her, even if they both kept all their clothes on. Which would make things easier, no question. "Just sit down. I'll start with your shoulders."

"Okay," she agreed, then returned her sponge to the sink and sat down at the table, where he gently pressed his fists against the tight muscles along the top of her shoulders. "Ooh. That's nice."

"Yeah." He should have done this more often, because they'd gotten out of the habit after the first year or so. "Good."

She let out a slow, deep breath, and he felt her skin growing warmer under his hands. Good, this was good. Just do this for her, just ease the tension from her shoulders...and it was working, he could tell during the next ten minutes as his fingers found and released the pressure points, because he could feel her relaxing under his touch.

"I wish," she murmured, "you could do this all night."

If they were making wishes, he'd wish for her to stay here. He knew better than to trust such fantasies, but as for wishing he could do this all night...

"So do I."

Maybe she heard the sadness in his voice, because she looked up at him behind her. "Rafe—"

"No, come on, don't tense up."

"You're making me tense," she muttered. Then, so softly he almost missed it, she continued, "You're making me want you."

Even now? Maybe it shouldn't surprise him, because she'd always enjoyed his massages, but he couldn't help feeling a tremor of pleasure. "Ah."

She leaned her head forward, inviting his hands to press deeper against her shoulder blades, and Rafe caught himself. He wasn't going to stop work yet. Not when he'd promised her a back rub.

Not unless she wanted something more.

And apparently she did, because after another few minutes of steady, gentle massage, she reached upward for his hands. "We could go to bed early," she said.

All right, that was clear enough. Wasn't it?

"We could," he agreed, keeping hold of one hand and using his other to rub the soft spot above her spine. One last time sounded wonderfully tempting…and painfully final. He already knew, from his memories of Rose, that there was nothing more agonizing than goodbye sex…and he hadn't loved Rose the way he loved Beth.

But no matter how much it might hurt, he couldn't resist one last time.

"We could go to bed," he murmured, "right now."

"Oh, yes," she breathed, and he gathered her into his arms. Carried her down the hall. Nothing else to think about, no thinking about goodbye or tomorrow or anything but Beth, right now, right here in his arms, his bed, right now.

Beth. Now. Always.

Always wonderful, yes, her softness, the way she moved against him, beneath him, around him, her little gasps, her astonishing warmth, her welcome and wonder and now, yes, Beth! This was who he loved, how he loved, and he would love her as long as he could, as hard as he could, just Beth with him, here, now, more, yes—

Yes.

Yes!

He heard her cry out, felt her convulse with the same joy that soared through him in a rush of heat and color and light, leaving him triumphant and empty and rejoicing and helpless and strong...the way she always did.

Always.

Beth.

"Yes," she whispered, and he felt his heart twist again as he gazed at her tangled amidst the sheets he would keep for as long as he could. "That was wonderful."

That was good. She was relaxed, anyway, and tomorrow he could take comfort in knowing he'd given her everything he could. Rafe drew her against him, closing his eyes while she nestled into his embrace, and fought to keep himself from wishing for more.

"Good," he answered softly, knowing she was so close to sleep that she wouldn't even hear him. "Because now, when you leave...at least you'll leave happy."

Chapter Eleven

At least he was happy. There was nothing her husband loved more than night-into-day meetings with gang leaders, and for his sake Beth had been glad he'd have such a compelling distraction while she was leaving for Chicago.

But that didn't make it much easier to wake up alone.

It must have been the sound of his car starting that woke her, because a glance at the clock showed he couldn't have been gone long. Rafe had always been skilled at silence, rising and showering and dressing so quietly that she rarely heard him taking off early.

So she shouldn't be disappointed that he'd managed it this morning. After all, she was the one who'd wanted to avoid a prolonged goodbye.

It was better this way.

Even so, she felt an embarrassing rush of gratitude when she made her way to the kitchen and found he'd left her a note on the table.

Nothing sentimental, she could tell before she even picked it up. He'd used the same scratch-pad paper they used for writing notes like "Call the office" or "Turn off the cook-pot," and his handwriting was the same slashing scrawl as ever.

But it made her throat tighten as she read the three simple lines.

You already know to call me if you need anything.
You already know I love you.
Always.

Beth swallowed against the rising tears, knowing she couldn't afford to start crying now. She had to keep up her spirit of independence if she was going to make this new life work.

She had to pretend she was someone like Anne— or even Anne herself—who could embark on a solo venture with all the confidence in the world.

So she forced herself to hum all the carefree tunes she could think of while starting the coffeemaker, getting ready for her travel day while it brewed, and returning to the kitchen for a leisurely ten-minute cup of coffee that would last until her shuttle arrived.

Only then, while gazing again at Rafe's note, did she notice how much thinner the notepad was.

He must have gone through forty sheets of paper while drafting that casual-looking goodbye.

A realization that warmed her.

Not that it mattered, but she couldn't resist peeking in the trash for evidence of his struggle at composition. Sure enough, there were dozens of crumpled pages.

And, lying on top of them, a medal.

She caught her breath.

This was Rafe's only token of security, and somehow it had wound up in the trash.

Her first thought was that it must have slipped out of his pocket, but even as she reached to pick it up she knew that couldn't have happened.

No, he had deliberately thrown it away.

Proving he didn't need it.

But who was he trying to convince? She already knew he didn't need anything or anyone.

Only...

Maybe Rafe didn't know that.

Maybe he didn't trust his own strength.

"The more I looked out for whoever needed it, the better I could handle everything else."

"I take care of people. I don't need people taking care of me."

"That's what it takes to survive."

Beth returned to her coffee, clutching the medal in her hand.

Survival.

After all these years, he was still worried about survival.

"I kept telling myself to quit hoping, get over it."

"I've never been any good at...at loving."

"I don't want you knocking yourself out for me."

How many times had he told her, and how many times had she refused to listen?

"Don't worry about me."

"I don't need security."

"I can take care of myself."

So what on earth was she doing, expecting him to need her?

But she already knew the answer. She had read it yesterday in Anne's journal, and now the quote about "Bethie" echoed in her sister's voice.

"She's always felt like she's no good unless somebody needs her."

So she knew perfectly well what she'd been doing.

She'd been using Rafe.

All this time.

Pinning her insecurities on him. Relying on him to make her feel worthwhile. Waiting for him to turn her into someone who mattered.

Instead of accepting him as the loner he was.

Instead of meeting *his* need to feel strong.

The sound of the shuttle arriving outside startled her. It couldn't be time to leave already—but, yes, the driver was right on schedule. She dumped the rest of her coffee down the sink, grabbed her purse and slid Rafe's note and medal inside, then went out to direct the driver in loading her suitcases and carry-on.

Too late to call him at the clinic now. Too late to apologize.

And if she tried, he would only tell her not to worry. He was fine. "You didn't hurt me," he would insist, and he would believe that with all his strength.

The strength she had steadily tried to ignore, in hopes that he would start leaning on her.

No wonder, she realized as the shuttle covered the endless miles toward the airport, he'd found it so easy living with the woman they thought was Anne.

As Anne, she had valued him exactly as he was.

But as Beth, she had never managed to do that.

And now, with the entire Dolls-Like-Me staff expecting her to make things work, it was too late to ask his forgiveness. Too late to honor his need for strength.

Too late to become the woman Rafe deserved.

She deserved more than a note, Rafe thought as he drove to Legalismo, but he knew better than to leave her a bouquet of flowers on the table.

Although maybe if he ordered some for when she arrived in Chicago, she'd enjoy that.

He could do this. He was okay. He could phone a florist, provide an address, do whatever he had to.

Because the pain right after a stabbing was never too intense. For the first few minutes, you didn't really feel anything.

Same when somebody walked out. Except in those cases, where you had some warning, the grace period lasted even longer. Usually a day or two while you kept walking around, acting normal, knowing you weren't and knowing there was nothing you could do except wait for the ache to crest, shatter you, tear you apart and—

And until then, you were fine.

He was fine. He could do whatever he had to.

Call a florist, right.

First things first, though, and it looked like Oscar had already arrived outside the clinic and started checking the windows. Squinting sideways at the shades, in case someone had taken a hiding place inside.

Same kind of precaution he would've taken at that

age, Rafe noted with a mixture of approval and regret. If he could just get Oscar off the streets...

"Cholo couldn't make it," the kid announced as soon as he started toward the door. "But he likes what you're doing for Billy."

So did Rafe. Cholo's cousin was going to be acquitted, and that would mean more people wanting help from the clinic. More opportunity to attract interns, to attract grants, to make Legalismo into the kind of place that had saved his life.

"Billy's gonna be fine," he told Oscar, wondering how many times he'd have to use that word today. But he *was* fine, and so was Billy. "You can tell that to anyone you want."

The kid shoved his hands into his pockets—no gun today, Rafe noticed—and waited for him to unlock the front door before sauntering inside with his usual edgy attitude. "Sure. Anyway, now Cholo told Gabe—you know, the guy on top—you're okay. And Gabe wants to talk to you about some other stuff."

Exactly what he'd hoped, because an endorsement from someone like that would carry far more weight than a social worker's. But Gabe would have to show up in person for the message to do any good.

"I'm around most of the time," Rafe answered, pocketing his keys and leading the way inside.

Oscar closed the door behind him and shifted from one foot to the other, studiously avoiding any glance at the No Drugs/No Weapons sign. "Yeah, but there's kind of a problem with that." He hesitated, as if searching for the most diplomatic way to explain what might be an unpleasant surprise. "See, nobody likes coming in where they can't defend themselves."

"I know." No point in mentioning that any un-armed kid was taking a big step toward trust. No point in glancing down the hall toward his office, where Beth's picture would still be sitting on the desk. "It takes guts."

Oscar looked faintly uncomfortable. "Uh…"

"Like you've got," Rafe said, and flicked on the light switch.

Then halted as the realization struck him.

The kid hadn't brought a gun, no. But the way he looked, he must be carrying a knife.

Rafe moved to open the door and gestured to him. "Outside."

To his credit, Oscar didn't even attempt a bluff. Instead he followed him outside and crossed his arms. "See, the thing is, I need it."

"On the street, yeah." No point in pretending the world was safe—people could attack any minute, same as people could leave—but he would guarantee the clinic's safety with his very life. "Not in here."

"Maybe not now, but you never know what'll come up."

No, you didn't. No matter how well you'd learned to defend yourself, there were always unexpected dangers.

Unexpected losses.

But he was fine. Focusing on the kid. Who'd just pointed out that you never knew what might come up…

Rafe sighed. "I know," he acknowledged, and reached back in the doorway to turn off the lights. No point burning electricity if Oscar wasn't coming inside. "I thought the same thing."

The kid shot him a startled glance, as if he'd forgotten they shared any common experience. "Yeah?"

"Long time ago." And the day he'd put aside his knife had been one of the biggest steps in his life. Far bigger than passing the bar exam, which was supposed to be the triumph of a lifetime. But back in his gang days— "You wouldn't get me anyplace without some kind of backup."

Oscar nodded, shoving his hands even deeper into his pockets. "Well, so you know how it is."

"Yeah, I know." In any case, there was no point just standing around outside the clinic, gazing at the door where Beth had hung his opening-day sign. Shoving the memory out of his mind, he slammed the door and locked it. "Let's go get some coffee."

They made their way to the bodega without seeing anyone except an elderly couple who crossed the street to avoid them, which made the kid stand taller. But on the way back, Oscar was so full of conversation about Bianca that Rafe had a hard time keeping his thoughts off Beth.

He could do whatever he had to, though.

He was fine.

"So," the kid asked with elaborate nonchalance as they reached the last block before the clinic, "when do you want Gabe to come by?"

"Anytime he wants." This was going to be a long and elaborate dance, but all he could do was go through the steps. "Long as he brings someone to stay outside with the weapons."

The kid faltered, and Rafe saw a momentary look of guilt on his face. Whether for not having thought of that solution himself or for having tried to sneak one past, he couldn't tell.

"Well, I'll let him know."

"Same for you. Anytime you want to come in."

Oscar reached toward his knife, as if ready to hand it over on the spot, then hesitated. Reconsidered. And nodded.

"Next time. Nothing against you, okay?" he muttered, and Rafe felt a tug of compassion. That was the closest he'd ever get to an apology, and it didn't come easy for a kid like this. "It's just, like you say, better having some kind of backup."

Yeah, he remembered that feeling. He took another sip of coffee, trying to come up with the right response.

Because if he couldn't reach this former self of his, if he couldn't make a difference to someone who needed it, he had wasted an awful lot of nights without Beth.

No, don't think about Beth.

Just explain the knife. Needing some kind of backup, remember?

Okay, he could answer that.

"Thing is, Oscar," he said, "if you're not enough without a weapon—and it took me a long time to realize this—you're not gonna be enough *with* it, either."

The kid stayed silent long enough that Rafe could tell he was digesting the thought. Then, as they reached the curb outside Legalismo, he raised an objection.

"It's different for you, though. You've got that shield."

His first image was of Beth's knight in shining armor, but he'd never even possessed a sword, much less a shield. "What?"

"I mean, it's kind of like a shield, you know?" Oscar explained, gesturing a force field in the air. "All the way around you."

That was actually a pretty good analogy, considering the guard he'd managed to build around the fears and weaknesses that could have brought him down. "Armor," he said, and the kid nodded.

"Yeah. Nobody's gonna get past that."

Nobody except Beth, who had worked her way past it the very first day they met.

But he didn't need thoughts of Beth right now.

Leaving him.

Wishing he were different.

Giving up hope that he could ever be what she wanted.

"So it's different for you," Oscar continued, sitting down on the curb as if to prove he accepted the rule about staying outside. "But I don't have that kind of armor."

No, all he had were the gang and the gun, and those were never enough. "It takes a while to build," Rafe said, sitting beside him and taking another gulp of coffee. "But once you've got it—"

"Yeah," the kid interrupted more enthusiastically than usual, "then people can come at you from all directions, and never get through."

From all directions.

"I'd be happy to listen."

"Is that what it takes to get you here? Me getting hurt?"

"I just keep trying, and I don't know what to do."

"If I had a shield," Oscar began, and Rafe cut him off.

"Bianca's probably glad you don't."

The kid shot him a baffled glance. "She doesn't want me getting hurt! And the right kind of armor, like you've got…nobody's gonna get past that."

Nobody.

Never.

Not even Beth.

"Maybe you've never noticed, but sometimes I feel like I'm in this marriage by myself."

"You don't let anybody take care of you."

"You don't need me. You don't need anyone."

But he couldn't need anyone. There was no faster way to lose people than by depending on them. Soon as you started needing someone, like a mom or grandpa or buddy or girlfriend, you might as well say goodbye.

Save yourself the heartache.

"It doesn't always work," Rafe muttered.

"What, the shield?" Oscar sounded intrigued, the way any kid would during a discussion of flaws in weapons. "My .38 jammed once, and I thought I was dead."

Dead was better than hurting, though.

At least the kind of hurting that came from watching someone walk off with your heart on a stick.

Rafe closed his eyes for a moment. "There's worse things," he said.

The kid looked baffled. "Huh?"

Maybe nobody had ever told him there were worse things than death. "Losing somebody," he explained, and felt the familiar ache rising in his chest, where it started every time. "Oscar, the shield doesn't always work. You can still get hurt."

"Not as bad, though."

Maybe not. Maybe without the shield, the ache of loss would have penetrated all the way through his chest by now.

Maybe that was the whole point of armor—protecting your heart.

Yeah, probably.

But with his heart so thoroughly protected, Rafe wondered, what exactly did that leave for Beth?

"You'd rather be with the kids than here." Lonely… *"I'm not who you want."*

Not enough.

Not nearly enough.

Because all this time he insisted he loved her, he'd been shutting her out with that shield.

Forcing her away.

Keeping his distance from the woman he loved.

And, God, he had a lot to make up for—if only he could.

Well, he could damn sure try.

Rafe stood up. "I've got to go," he told Oscar, and tossed the last of his coffee onto the street. "I've gotta find my wife at the airport."

"She goes a lot of places," the kid observed, looking at him curiously. Probably anyone within ten feet could see the panic building in his veins, Rafe realized, but there was no point in explaining it now.

"I need to get her back," he said, and started for his car with Oscar a few steps behind him. "I *need* her."

"What, she's got your keys?"

The question almost made him laugh—trust a kid to think of the only urgent reason a man might need his wife—but he found himself trying to explain as he fumbled to unlock the car door.

"No. No, I mean, I need her. I've been saying I didn't need anyone, but Beth—" Ask for another chance. Take the risk. "Loving her isn't enough," he blurted, "and she saw that all along. I've got to get her back."

Oscar evidently recognized the gravity of the situation, because he offered a parting piece of advice as Rafe got into the car. "Maybe you need to give her some flowers."

"No." He started the motor, pulled into Reverse, and told the kid the truth. "This time, I need to give her myself."

"Can't you go any faster?" Beth asked the shuttle driver, and he shot her a dark glance.

"Not unless you want to get stuck in a pothole. This isn't the best part of town, all right?"

No, she knew that. But the sense of urgency about seeing Rafe, which had made her order a retreat from the airport, was growing stronger with every passing minute.

"There," she said, pointing toward the next Stop sign. "Down that street." Surely Rafe would still be at the clinic, rather than in court or out talking to clients.

Because she had to reach him fast.

She had to make him see that he mattered more

than anything, and the only way to do that was by finding him now.

Only two more blocks to Legalismo, and—yes, there. Oh, he was there! Talking to some kid who must be Oscar, unlocking the door of his car, and—

No, he couldn't be leaving. Beth rolled down the window and called his name, earning another muffled curse from the shuttle driver.

But he couldn't hear her, she realized, because the car was starting to move.

Toward the back side of the parking lot, away from her.

"Oscar," she cried desperately, and the boy looked in her direction as she pointed to Rafe's car. "Stop him!"

He reacted with impressive speed, racing after Rafe as the driver screeched to a halt. "Ma'am," he said, "hold on. You've got to—"

"Just a minute!" She flung herself out of the shuttle and ran across the parking lot, only to find Rafe slamming the car door and hurrying toward her.

"Are you all right?" he demanded.

The look of concern in his eyes, the tension in his body shamed her. If he couldn't imagine her seeking him out except for help, she had so much to make up for.

"Rafe," she blurted, throwing her arms around him, "I had to come tell you—"

He began speaking at almost the same moment, even as he pulled her into his embrace. "I was on my way—"

"I've been so wrong." She had to explain that first and let him get back to whatever he'd been doing that made him look so frantic, but somehow she couldn't seem to get the words out fast enough. "I've been waiting for you to make me into someone who matters," she stammered, "and that's not your job."

"Beth—"

"That's *my* job." And if it weren't for Anne's journal and his discarded medal, it would have taken her far longer to realize that truth. "I should've been doing more for the Down syndrome girls all along, the way I used to, instead of trying to make you need me."

"I do need you," he said, just as the shuttle driver called from the sidewalk.

"Ma'am, I've got your luggage."

She couldn't deal with that yet, but already Rafe was pulling some bills from his pocket and gesturing to the boy near the clinic door.

"Oscar, take care of that guy, will you?"

No, wait, she hadn't finished her apology. She hadn't even started it, and here he was taking her arm as if everything was forgiven, as if all he wanted was her coming inside with him.

And with the two other kids she saw sauntering toward the door, followed by a college girl who must be the newest intern. He had a life waiting for him, and she needed to let him take care of everyone else, but—

"I just have to tell you all this," Beth pleaded, "before I mess it up."

He stopped in the middle of a breath, as if he'd been ready to interrupt her, and rested both his hands on her shoulders. "Okay," he said, and she could see in his eyes a mixture of anticipation and uneasiness.

Which left her feeling even more frazzled. "You can talk first, but I've got something to say, too."

Oscar called from the sidewalk, where the shuttle driver was unloading her suitcases, "Want your stuff inside?"

There was too much going on, too much to deal with, but Rafe didn't seem at all distracted.

"Yeah," he told the boy, reaching for his keys and throwing them across the parking lot in a graceful arc. Then, as Oscar caught the keys, he turned back to her. "Let's get out of here."

But that was what she'd come to tell him, that she understood why the clinic mattered so much. That she no longer expected him to put her first, time and time again.

"No," she protested, "this is where you belong."

"I belong with you," he said simply. "Wherever you are."

She couldn't remember him ever saying that before, and it lifted her heart for a moment. But she hadn't yet asked him for a chance to rebuild their marriage.

"Well," Beth said, "I'm staying right here." Right in the middle of the Legalismo parking lot, for as long as it took to make her pledge of atonement. "Because I need to tell you how sorry I am. All this time, I wanted you to *need* me, and I didn't care about anything else." Just hurry, just get the request out. "But, Rafe, if you can forgive me...if we can start over..."

He gazed at her silently, his expression one she'd never seen before, and she felt a tremor of hope. Fear. Maybe a little of each. "Wanna go for a walk?" he asked.

"Okay," she said, and they started across the parking lot toward the quieter street. Suggesting a walk had to be a good sign, right? If he didn't want to start over, wouldn't he say so right now?

No, she realized as he reached for her hand, he wouldn't. Rafe would do whatever he could to accommodate any request she made, same as he'd done when she tried getting him to talk.

And if he didn't truly want her in his life, he would never say that in so many words.

"Can I talk now?" he asked.

Nor would he interrupt after giving her the right to talk first, she knew. Oh, but please, let this man want to start over.

Please, let him understand.

"Yes," she managed to answer.

He stopped walking, and moved a few feet sideways so his shadow blocked her from the sun. Then he took a long breath, and faced her straight.

"None of this," he said, "was your fault. None of it."

She stared at him.

"I've been telling myself all this time," Rafe continued, "I don't need anyone, but that was wrong." He hesitated, then lifted his hands in a gesture of relinquishment. "I need you."

Two days ago she would have taken that statement as a joyous victory, as a cause for celebration, but now she knew the difference between nurturing from compulsion and nurturing from love. Even so, the thought of him needing her was unbearably sweet. "You don't have to," she whispered.

"I know, but I can't help it." He reached for her

hands, still watching her intently. "Beth, I kept trying to shut you out, keep this armor on—"

"And that's okay," she interrupted. He could wear all the armor he needed, if that's what it took for him to survive. "I love you the way you are."

Rafe caught his breath.

Blinked a few times.

Started to speak.

Blinked again, and she saw a glimmer of moisture at the corner of his eyes as he fumbled for words.

She had never once told her husband, Beth realized as she saw him swallow hard, that she loved him exactly the way he was.

That she accepted him for who he was.

The way she had when they thought she was Anne.

"You know," she told him, "for that month after the train wreck, I was doing everything right. I quit *using* you, expecting you to make me feel important…and that's something I should have figured out a long time ago."

He shook his head, as if dismissing any error on her part. "No, it was my fault. I was scared of needing you, but I've always needed you. I was wrong."

"All right, we were both wrong." They could share the blame, and they could share the fresh start as well. "I was being all grabby and clingy, and you were being a…a rock. But from now on, we can both lean on each other."

Rafe grinned, moving beside her and tilting his body against hers until she laughed and leaned on him, as well. "We can depend on each other," he agreed, straightening up and putting his arm around her shoulders as they started walking again. "Need each other. Want each other."

All of that, yes, which added up to a heartwarming conclusion. "Love each other."

"And," he said softly, "our children."

Oh, this was too much happiness. This was everything she'd wished for, all spread out before her like a dazzling shower of joy.

"We can wait for having children," Beth told him, and saw his look of surprise. "Seriously. That was just me trying to be important, not even considering how much the clinic matters to you."

With a careless gesture at the building behind him, he dismissed Legalismo in a single wave. "It doesn't matter like you do."

He'd said that before, she remembered, but this time was different.

This time, when she no longer needed him to make her important, she knew he was telling the truth.

"But the street kids—"

"They're important, yeah, but they're not my family." Rafe stopped again, turning to look at her directly. "You are."

She felt another rush of wonder coursing through her, making her blood dance. "And you're mine. That's why I don't mind waiting."

He nodded slowly, and met her gaze with an expression that seemed almost shy. "Okay, maybe this is selfish of me, but I like having somebody I can love this much. That's why I want…more."

More family.

More people to love.

She couldn't imagine a more perfect reason to have children.

"So do I," Beth said, and leaned up to kiss him. A promise, a plan. A baby. "But now it's not because I have to nurture somebody. It's because I want to."

From the way he smiled at her, she could tell he understood the difference. "I want you nurturing our family," he said simply. "*And* me." Then, looking startled, he broke off. "I never thought I'd say that."

Neither had she, but that reminded her of the medal in her purse. "Speaking of nurturing," Beth said, and handed it to him. "I know you probably don't need this, but I saved it anyway. In case you changed your mind."

He looked from the medal to her, and before he could speak Oscar came sauntering across the parking lot.

"Your suitcases are inside," he told her. Then, to Rafe, "Heidi said she has to leave at noon."

Real life again. But so much sweeter than before. She watched with her blood still humming as Rafe showed Oscar the medal in his hand.

"Here's what got me through a couple of wars, back in L.A."

The boy gazed at it with a look of reverence. "That's the kind of thing," he observed, "people give their kids."

Rafe nodded, and when he glanced her way she could see the question in his eyes. And then, when she nodded a quick confirmation, he handed the medal to Oscar.

"With Beth and me on their side," he announced,

"our kids will have a lot going for them. I'd like you to have this."

The boy stared at him in amazement, then swallowed. "Thanks," he said, turning the medal in his hands. "This is kind of...powerful. You sure you don't need it?"

Rafe's serious expression gave way to a smile. "Yeah, I'm sure," he answered, and pulled Beth closer to him for another kiss. Another pledge. A promise of happiness, for them and their children to come. "We've got everything we need, right here."

Epilogue

They had everything they needed, Rafe knew. But he couldn't seem to stop pacing the hospital gift shop, looking for something to brighten Beth's eyes as soon as he found her in the new room.

With their daughter in her arms.

Only, what, eight more minutes to wait?

It felt like hours since he'd left the delivery room with a report for everyone waiting in the lobby, and he was still trembling from the relief of sharing the news that Beth and the baby were fine. That already they were being transferred upstairs, while he hurried to make his announcement and then ducked into the gift shop, wondering how the nurse had calculated when they'd be ready for him.

For their first moments as a family. Just Beth, himself and the baby.

Who still didn't seem quite real. Because with all the flurried activity in the delivery room, he didn't really feel like he'd been with his daughter.

Or even his wife.

Maybe he should bring her some flowers. Or a teddy bear. Or...

"I don't want flowers. I just want you."

Rafe set down the flowers and started upstairs. He could wait in the hallway for another eight minutes, but he wanted to see Beth as soon as he could.

And when he got to the nurses' station outside her room, they waved him in so quickly that he knew she'd been asking for him.

He almost stumbled when he crossed the doorstep, because the sight of her holding their child hit him with unexpected impact. Beth looked so much better than when he'd left her in the delivery room, almost shining with joy as she turned the baby to face him, that Rafe felt himself reeling at the sight of her.

And their child.

So tiny.

So incredible.

So lovely, with her face all scrunched up and the little wisps of pale hair at the very top of her head. With her fragile little fists crossed across her chest. With an expression of bemusement that reflected his own so closely that he had a hard time catching his breath.

"She's beautiful," he whispered.

Beth's smile seemed to shimmer until he blinked a few times. Then she turned her face upward for his kiss, and he saw everything clearly again.

"Someday," she said in a dreamy voice, "I'm going to tell her that's the first thing you said when you saw her.''

Their daughter might not believe it during those teenage-angst years, but he knew it would always be true. And Beth seemed to know it, too, because she looked more contented than he'd ever seen her.

A welcome change from the last time he'd seen her. But that memory no longer seemed so frightening, so desperate, now that she was safe.

''I should've asked if you're okay,'' Rafe said.

''I'm still floating,'' she answered, then gave him the wry smile he loved. ''And you're still taking care of me.''

Maybe she didn't need it, but he would never stop taking care of her. ''You *and* our daughter, now,'' he told her, kneeling down for a face-to-face look at the baby. ''Hello, *niña*.''

Even though her sleepy expression didn't change, he felt a swift jolt of recognition. His child. His flesh and blood. And the feeling was so strong that Beth's voice seemed to come from a long distance away. ''Will you teach her to speak Spanish?''

''Sure, if she wants,'' he managed to answer. Then, realizing he couldn't even talk while gazing at their daughter, he straightened up again. ''I want to give her…everything,'' he muttered, hoping Beth would understand the fierce, primitive desire to cherish, to protect, to shower this child with all the good in the world. ''You know?''

''I know,'' she said, and from her misty-eyed expression he could tell that she understood it completely. ''I feel the same way. But first, we need to give her a name.''

They had decided to wait until the baby arrived before choosing a name, but had agreed that it should be for someone they loved. "I still like Anne," he said.

Beth swallowed, cradling the baby a little closer. "So do I." She had protested earlier that it wasn't fair to him if the name came from someone so much closer to her, but Rafe was determined to honor her favorite. "Really, would that be all right with you?"

"Sure. Anne was special." If for no other reason than her sister's continued affection. "Not like you, but—"

"If it weren't for her," Beth interrupted with a soft smile, "we wouldn't be here now."

What, in a hospital room? He was glad, Rafe realized, that this room was so different from the one where he'd worked to keep from flinching at the sight of her train-wreck bruises. "How's that?"

"When I thought I was her, remember?" She nuzzled the baby's forehead with her own, then looked up at him with the same contented expression he'd seen on the Madonna in church. "That's what showed me the difference between using you and loving you."

It was a change that had lasted over the past year, not only on her part but on his, as well. He no longer felt pressed to share Legalismo stories with her, yet by now it seemed like, every day on the way home, he couldn't wait to join Beth for dinner and conversation. About the people flowing into the clinic. About the street kids she'd started hiring for her business.

And if that was all because of Anne—

"We owe her a lot."

Beth's eyes misted over. "I wish she could see her niece."

But he knew that, if only from her twin's stories, Anne would always be a loving presence in this child's life.

"She can," Rafe said hoarsely, and reached for the baby. Lifting her in his arms, he spoke her name for every loving spirit to hear. "Anne Elizabeth Montoya."

Anne Elizabeth Montoya snuggled against him, and he felt his heart skip a beat.

Oh, God.

Our daughter.

Thank you. Thank you.

"You're going to be such a great father," he heard Beth say, and choked back a sudden lump in his throat.

To be a father to this baby...

"She's perfect," he breathed.

"She is," Beth agreed, and in her voice he heard the same awe that radiated through him. "Oh, and she got her first present."

They had already gotten dozens at the shower arranged by Beth's girlfriends, who had surprised everyone by inviting the Legalismo crew and the Down syndrome girls she'd stayed in touch with. But when she nodded at a white-ribboned package on the bedside table, he realized this was the baby's first present since birth. "No kidding?"

"The nurse dropped it off, from Oscar and Bianca. Isn't that sweet?"

He had canceled a meeting with Oscar when Beth

went into labor, but he'd never expected such a response. And Beth seemed to realize that he didn't want to set down the baby long enough to deal with wrappings, because she opened the box, fumbled with the tissue and held up a shining silver medal.

Exactly like the one he'd given Oscar last year.

Because he no longer needed it.

"That's lovely," Beth said softly, then opened the card and showed it to him.

"For the baby," Rafe read aloud, hoping his voice would stay steady, "who'll have everything she needs."

"They're absolutely right." Again the look of complacent certainty, which left him marveling at their daughter's good fortune. "She will."

But, as much as he wished otherwise, he already knew that was impossible. This child, like every other, would see her share of heartache no matter how fiercely he tried to protect her.

"Aw, Beth," he said, snuggling the baby closer as if to compensate for that failure. "We can't give her everything."

"We can give her the most important things, though." She smiled at him and the baby, dazzling him again with her expression of confidence. "A father who knows how to share, and how to be strong."

For strength, though, their daughter couldn't ask for a better model than Beth. "A mother who can run a company while she's eight months pregnant...and who nurtures better than anybody in the world."

And that was only the start of the important things, he realized when Beth gestured to the card from Oscar and Bianca. "Friends who care about her. Because her dad is making a difference for them."

It had been five months since he'd gotten the kid into that work/study program, but he couldn't claim a success just yet. "Still a long way to go."

"There always is," she agreed, with the easy practicality that had amazed him when he finally started sharing the gritty details of his work. "But I bet Oscar is going to turn out just like you."

"Yeah, maybe." That would be cause for pride, all right, but nothing compared to the pride of holding this child in his arms. Watching the steady rhythm of her chest, feeling the very pulse of her breath. "I hope," he said, "*she* turns out just like you."

"I know we can't give her everything," Beth admitted, lifting her gaze from the baby to him. "But if she can just find someone like you to love…she'll have what matters most."

Rafe swallowed. "Like I do."

"Like *we* do," she said, and the happiness in her voice made him wonder whether he could possibly take her into his arms. Yeah, as long as he set Anne on her lap. "Both of us."

"All three of us, now." Nestling the baby against him, he moved back toward his love. "Come on, Annie. Let's go kiss your mom."

* * * * *

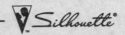

SPECIAL EDITION™

Coming in November to
Silhouette Special Edition
The fifth book in the exciting continuity

DARK SECRETS. OLD LIES. NEW LOVES.

THE MARRIAGE ACT

(Silhouette Special Edition #1646)

by

Elissa Ambrose

Plain-Jane accountant Linda Mailer had never done anything shocking in her life—until she had a one-night stand with a sexy detective and found herself pregnant! *Then* she discovered that her anonymous Romeo was none other than Tyler Carlton, the man spearheading the investigation of her beleaguered boss, Walter Parks. Tyler wanted to give his child a real family, and convinced Linda to marry him. Their passion sparked in close quarters, but Linda was wary of Tyler's motives and afraid of losing her heart. Was he using her to get to Walter—or had they found the true love they'd both longed for?

Available at your favorite retail outlet.

If you enjoyed what you just read,
then we've got an offer you can't resist!

Take 2 bestselling
love stories FREE!
Plus get a FREE surprise gift!

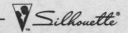

SPECIAL EDITION™

presents

bestselling author

Susan Mallery's

next installment of

Watch how passions flare
under the hot desert sun
for these rogue sheiks!

THE SHEIK & THE PRINCESS BRIDE

(SSE #1647, available November 2004)

Flight instructor Billie Van Horn's sexy
good looks and charming personality blew
Prince Jefri away from the moment he met
her. Their mutual love burned hot, but when
the Prince was suddenly presented with an
arranged marriage, Jefri found himself unable
to love the woman he had or have the
woman he loved. Could Jefri successfully
trade tradition for true love?

Available at your favorite retail outlet.

COMING NEXT MONTH

SPECIAL EDITION

#1645 CARRERA'S BRIDE—Diana Palmer
Long, Tall Texans
Jacobsville sweetheart Delia Mason was swept up in a tidal wave of trouble while on a tropical island holiday getaway. Luckily for this vulnerable small-town girl, formidable casino tycoon Marcus Carrera swooped in to the rescue. Their mutual attraction sizzled from the start, but could this tempestuous duo survive the forces conspiring against them?

#1646 THE MARRIAGE ACT—Elissa Ambrose
The Parks Empire
Red-haired beauty Linda Mailer didn't want her unexpected pregnancy to tempt Tyler Dalton into a pity proposal. But the green-eyed cop convinced Linda that, at least for the child's sake, a temporary marriage was in order. Their loveless marriage was headed for wedded bliss when business suddenly got in the way of their pleasure....

#1647 THE SHEIK & THE PRINCESS BRIDE—
Susan Mallery
Desert Rogues
From the moment they met, flight instructor Billie Van Horn's sexy good looks and charming personality blew Prince Jefri away. Their mutual love burned hot, but when Jefri was suddenly presented with an arranged marriage, he found himself unable to love the woman he had—or have the woman he loved. Could Jefri successfully trade tradition for true love?

#1648 A BABY ON THE RANCH—Stella Bagwell
Men of the West
When Lonnie Corteen agreed to search for his best friend's long-lost sister, he found the beautiful Katherine McBride pregnant, alone and in no mood to have her heart trampled on again. But Lonnie wanted to reunite her family—and become a part of it.

#1649 WANTED: ONE FATHER—Penny Richards
Single dad Max Murdock needed a quiet place to write and a baby-sitter for his daughter. Zoe Barlow had a cabin to rent and needed some extra cash. What began as a perfect match blossomed into the perfect romance. But could this lead to one big perfect family?

#1650 THE WAY TO A WOMAN'S HEART—Carol A. Voss
Nan Kramer had lost one man in the line of fire and wasn't about to put herself and her three children through losing another. Family friend—and local deputy—David Elliot agreed that because of his high-risk job, he should remain unattached. Nonetheless, David had found his way into this woman's heart, and neither wanted to send him packing....

SSECNM1004